ONE NIGHT OF SCANDAL

DARCY BURKE

ONE NIGHT OF SCANDAL

This is an UNCORRECTED PROOF for the purposes of advance review.

This book will be released on May 28, 2019

Don't miss any of the Wicked Dukes Club!

Have you read my other historical romance series?

The Untouchables featuring Society's most elite bachelors and the indomitable wallflowers, spinsters, and bluestockings who bring them to their knees.

Secrets and Scandals—the first book, Her Wicked Ways, is free!

Legendary Rogues featuring intrepid heroines and adventurous heroes on exciting quests for treasure (and love!) across Regency England and Wales!

Love romance? Have a free book (or two or three) on me!

Sign up at http://www.darcyburke.com/readerclub for members-only exclusives, including advance notice of pre-orders and insider scoop, as well as contests, giveaways, freebies, and 99 cent deals!

Want to share your love of my books with like-minded readers? Want to hang with me and get inside scoop? Then don't miss my exclusive Facebook groups!

Darcy's Duchesses for historical readers
Burke's Book Lovers for contemporary readers

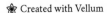

CHAPTER 1

LONDON, APRIL 1817

"*Tavistock!*"

Lady Viola Fairfax grinned at the welcome shouted by the men seated about the main salon of the Wicked Duke tavern, making the new faux whiskers glued to her cheeks pull against her skin. The discomfort of her gentleman's disguise scarcely registered after two years, but the sideburns had required replacement, as they did from time to time.

After exchanging pleasantries with a few of the regular customers, Viola took a seat at a table. Almost immediately, one of the barmaids, Prudence, deposited a tankard of ale in front of her. Prudence narrowed her gaze in a sly expression, and Viola wondered—not for the first time—if she'd guessed Tavistock was a woman.

It wouldn't surprise Viola. In fact, any surprise would lie in the fact that she was still fooling everyone. Well, everyone but her brother and his best friend, who owned the tavern.

She'd revealed her identity—secretly—to Val the

first night she'd appeared as Tavistock. He'd been shocked to learn she planned to dress as a man in order to report on the happenings at the Wicked Duke for the *Ladies' Gazette*. Initially, he'd tried to dissuade her, but it hadn't taken more than five minutes for her to convince him that she needed to do it, that writing would fill a void in her life.

While he'd understood and even supported her, he'd insisted she let his partner, the Duke of Colehaven, in on the secret. As the owners of the Wicked Duke, they were responsible for what happened there, and since they opened the doors to any and every one with peaceable intent, they should both know if Val's sister was masquerading as a man. Especially because she planned to do so on a regular basis.

Viola sipped her beer. As usual, Cole had crafted a masterful brew. Unless his wife had created the recipe. Viola smiled to herself, thinking it must have been Diana.

"Langford!" came the next greeting as Giles Langford entered the tavern.

Langford, a blacksmith who was every bit as comfortable driving a vehicle as he was building one, sat down to her left. "Ho there, Tavistock. Haven't seen you in a few weeks."

"Been busy." Pitching her voice to Tavistock's lower octave was second nature.

"Time for another column, eh?" Langford sipped his ale. "Does anyone actually read the nonsense you write?"

He was referring to her, rather S. D. Tavistock's, well-known column in the *Ladies' Gazette*, a monthly magazine. Viola worked to keep her tone even despite Langford's irritating question as she swung her gaze toward his. "What makes you think it's nonsense?"

"I didn't mean any offense. I just assumed you didn't write what actually happens here, so I meant literal nonsense." He shrugged.

"You don't read it, then." Viola snorted before taking a drink.

Langford laughed. "Why on earth would I read the *Ladies' Gazette*?"

He had a point there. Viola could barely stomach reading it. The articles were written by men but directed at women, as if they were qualified to know what a woman might want to read. In fact, the entire magazine was produced—idiotically—by men. When Viola had first inquired about writing for them, they'd firmly informed her they did not hire women. Furthermore, they'd seemed horrified by the prospect. One would have thought she was some sort of monster instead of the very audience they were trying to reach.

On a lark, she'd tried again a month later. If they only hired men, she'd give them what they wanted.

She went the second time as Samuel Darius Tavistock, bachelor extraordinaire with an inside look on the happenings of the Wicked Duke, London's most notorious tavern owned by two dukes and frequented by all walks of society, from the peerage right on down to the blacksmith seated beside Viola. The publisher had delighted in Tavistock's idea for "Observations on Gentlemen," and the column had appeared monthly for the past two years.

While it gave her the opportunity to write *something*, it wasn't what Viola wanted to be doing. She wanted to write something important.

She'd started a dozen manuscripts and hadn't finished one. She'd drafted pamphlets addressing voting inequality and the steep divide between wealthy landowners and impoverished workers, but those had gone unpublished. Perhaps it was time she considered publishing them on her own. Surely Val would help her.

Or not.

Her pamphlets could potentially cause trouble for Val, given his responsibilities in the House of Lords. If anyone knew the Duke of Eastleigh's sister wrote and published pamphlets advocating reform, there would be a scandal. And never mind how it might affect Val or Viola. Their grandmother would suffer a fit of apoplexy.

Returning to Langford's comment, Viola had to admit he was right. She did write nonsense. Not in the sense that it was fictional, but it *was* silly in the larger scheme of things. Who cared how gentlemen behaved when they were together in a tavern?

A pair of gentlemen came in to the chorus of "Caldwell!" and "Sir Humphrey!" Members of Parliament, they were two of many MPs who frequented the Wicked Duke. Instead of sitting, they went to the bar where Doyle, the barkeep, gave them each an ale.

Caldwell, a tall, thin man with sharp blue eyes, always made Viola think of a predator. He seemed to assess every situation for vulnerability; at least that was how he made her feel. Sir Humphrey was far more affable, often joking and eager to make those around him laugh. He softened Caldwell's edges, making the man somewhat palatable, and since they were nearly always together, Viola had often wondered if that was the reason why Caldwell had befriended him.

Sir Humphrey turned toward the table. "Evening, lads. Good to see you, Tavistock. Seems as though it's been a while. Must be time for another column. Let's see if I can think of something sensational for you to include." He tapped his finger against his thin lips.

"I'm merely observing," Viola said. "If you tell me something outright, it's not quite as authentic." And yet he did it every single time she saw him. Clearly, he was angling for a mention in the column. Perhaps she'd satisfy his desperation this month. "Unless it's something the readers of the *Ladies' Gazette* simply *must* know."

"The Viscount Orford is looking for a wife." Sir Humphrey waggled his brows. "You heard it from me first."

Caldwell rolled his eyes. "Ignore him," he said crisply. Then he shot Viola a look tinged with...humor? "Come, old man." Caldwell dragged Sir Humphrey who wasn't "old," but probably only a decade more than Viola's twenty-six years, into the private salon where more intimate conversations could be held.

Langford narrowed his eyes at them and snorted as they left. "Probably coming up with new ideas to cheat the working class." He polished off his ale and stood.

Viola looked up at him. "Before you go, any races coming up I can mention in my column?"

Giles Langford was precisely the type of man the readers of the *Ladies' Gazette* wanted to read about. With his golden hair, bone-melting smile, and skill with the whip, he made ladies of all ages and status swoon. It didn't matter that he wasn't titled or wealthy. He was handsome, and he won every race he competed in. That was a man women dreamed about.

But not Viola. She didn't dream of men at all.

"Stop by Rotten Row at dawn this Saturday if you want to see Adolphus Fernsby burst into tears," Langford offered, his hazel eyes sparkling. In *ton* gatherings, Fernsby was a nuisance at best. On the racetrack, he was even worse—infamous for self-important speeches about why he, his carriage, and his horses were better than everyone else's.

"Whom will he be racing?" she asked.

Langford grinned. "Me."

Viola couldn't help but return his smile. She had no doubt most of the men in this tavern would be there to cheer on one of their own.

Viola lifted her tankard toward him. "Thank you for the tip." Langford inclined his head before departing.

After chatting with a few other gentlemen while she nursed her ale, Viola eventually stood and went into the private salon. This was where she typically overheard gossip that might be of interest to the readers of the *Ladies' Gazette*.

Several of the tables in the salon were occupied by two, three, and four gentlemen. She swept her gaze over the room, mentally cataloging those present, most of whom were known to her. Gregory Pennington, another MP, came in behind her. He was a larger fellow—thick in the middle with what seemed to be a disappearing neck—and she had to step farther into the room to make way for him. She followed him with her eyes as he wound his way to Sir Humphrey and Caldwell's table. The three men's heads tipped toward the center as they began speaking in an animated fashion.

Two popular gentlemen, the Marquess of Raymore and the Viscount Keswick, sat at a table, laughing. Viola made her way in that direction and took up a position near the hearth so she could hear at least snippets of their conversation. They were discussing what was on the lips of many people at present: the new seditious meetings law.

"Careful there," Keswick said with a laugh. "If someone says the wrong thing at a ball, it might be against the law!"

Both men chuckled as Viola sipped her beer. The law was horrible, but everyone was in a heightened state of distress after the riot in December and the attack on the Prince Regent in January—all the responsibility of radicals who met en masse and apparently plotted mayhem. Or so some believed.

Sir Humphrey and Caldwell stood and left, and Pennington transferred himself to Raymore and Keswick's table. His gaze wandered, and a moment later, his small, dark eyes settled on Viola. "Tavistock, come join us!" he invited.

She looked toward Raymore and Keswick, since Pennington had sat down uninvited and was now encouraging her to join them. "If you don't mind?"

"Not at all," Keswick said, gesturing to the remaining open chair. "Good to see you, Tavistock. Dare we speak freely now that you've arrived, or shall we expect our utterances to appear in the *Ladies' Gazette*?" He laughed, and the other two gentlemen smiled in response.

"I am always kind," Viola said, flourishing her hand. "Unless someone deserves to have their true nature revealed." She narrowed her eyes at them and chuckled, which elicited more laughter from Keswick.

"Best not get on Tavistock's bad side, eh, Pennington?" Keswick elbowed Pennington.

Pennington slid her an arrogant smile. "Bah, I'm not concerned about what he might write for a *women's* publication."

Now Viola would definitely try to find something to write about him.

Pennington sniffed. "Far more important things happening than whose cravat needs more starch." As if *that* was what Viola was writing about. Except sometimes, it was.

"Then give me something more important to write about," she dared, staring him in the eye.

Pennington shot a look toward Raymore, then curled his hand around his tankard. "All right.

There's a rumor that a certain MP has aligned himself with the radicals."

Keswick waved a hand. "There are plenty of MPs who sympathize with that lot."

"Sympathy is one thing, but when they take steps to aid them…" Pennington lifted a shoulder. "That's something different entirely."

Viola's pulse tripped over itself. "Are you saying there's an MP who helped them? How?"

"Didn't you say it was a rumor?" Raymore asked. At Pennington's nod, the marquess picked up his ale. "Then it's probably best not to spread gossip."

"But Tavistock here deals in gossip," Keswick said, winking in Viola's direction.

If there were any truth to this rumor, it would transcend "gossip." Viola's mind worked. How could she find out?

Pennington rose. "Well, I'm off to Brooks's. Cheers!" He picked up his mug and strolled back to the main parlor.

Raymore shook his head. "No one would be foolish enough to help the radicals. Not now after all that's happened."

Viola agreed the MP would be a fool. Habeas corpus had been suspended last month, and anyone could be imprisoned for any reason. It was a dangerous time for those who sought change and equality.

"Perhaps he did it before," Keswick mused. "As I said, there are plenty of MPs who some see as 'radical.' Burdett, for one."

Viola filed the name away. She suddenly stood. "Excuse me, gentlemen, I must mingle." In truth, she was keen to leave…

As she made her way back toward the main salon, she had to stop short before running straight into her brother, Valentine Fairfax, the Duke of Eastleigh.

Val's blond brows pitched over his green eyes. "Tavistock, I didn't realize you would be here tonight." Though he kept his voice low, he still addressed her by the fake name.

"Just on my way out, actually."

Val stepped toward the corner, and she felt she had to follow. He lowered his voice even further. "You're supposed to tell me when you plan to come in."

"And tear you away from Isabelle?" Viola referred to his new wife, whom he adored. "I'm not about to disrupt your newfound—and well-deserved —happiness."

"It's not as if I don't come in here just about every day."

"I know, but you don't spend as much time here as you did. Neither does Cole. Too busy enjoying being married. As you should be."

Val frowned. "We had an agreement. If you're going to continue this deception, you'll do it under my supervision."

She gave him an apologetic smile. "You aren't always here, and I have a column to write. Anyway, I'm leaving. I promise I'll inform you next time."

"Where is Grandmama?" Val asked.

Viola resided with their grandmother and occasionally went out with her in the evening, depending on her destination. Most of the time, however, Viola preferred to stay home—or come to the Wicked Duke. "At a card party."

"If she only knew…" Val breathed.

"She never will." Viola glanced over the salon to see if anyone noted their whispered conversation in the corner. They didn't appear to.

"Perhaps it's time you cease this behavior. Every time you dress as Tavistock, you risk being discovered."

"After all this time, I highly doubt that would happen. However, we're drawing attention standing here whispering. I'm going now. Give my love to Isabelle."

"I will. Go straight home," he said.

Viola nodded, then she walked into the main salon and deposited her tankard on the bar. After bidding good night to Doyle, she left the tavern and hailed a hack.

"Where to?" the driver asked.

Anticipation curled through her as she contemplated her destination. "Brooks's."

CHAPTER 2

*J*ack Barrett stepped out of Brooks's, anxious to be on his way. If not for the meeting one of his fellow MPs had arranged, he would've skipped the club entirely. He much preferred the informal and convivial atmosphere at the Wicked Duke.

"Thank you for coming tonight," Viscount Orford said from behind him, drawing Jack to turn. Orford had been part of the meeting. Though they didn't always see eye to eye—Orford was from a rotten borough and didn't appreciate Jack speaking out against them—they often found themselves working on the same committees.

Jack pushed out a breath. "I fear it was a waste of time."

"I do not. Any occasion we attempt to breach our political differences is well spent." Orford, a muscular fellow, clapped him on the shoulder with zeal. "I look forward to our next debate."

"As do I." Jack turned, intending to move onto the pavement, and nearly collided with Gregory Pennington, an MP whose titled grandfather was the sole reason he possessed a membership to Brooks's.

"Evening, Barrett," he greeted. "You aren't on your way out, are you?"

"I am, in fact. My meeting has concluded."

Pennington's dark eyes widened. "Meeting? I hope there weren't more than fifty of you." He chortled as if the Seditious Meetings Act was a jest instead of an abomination.

Jack gritted his teeth. "There were not. Once you go inside, you will note, however, that there are at least fifty persons in the subscription room."

"But they're talking and gambling, not discussing grievances."

Arching a brow, Jack decided to provoke the man. "Are you saying we were raising grievances in our meeting?"

"I was joking," Pennington said, pouting. "You've no sense of humor on this topic, I see."

"None. Now, if you'll excuse me, I'm for the Wicked Duke." Which was where Jack usually encountered Pennington.

"Just came from there." Pennington focused on something beyond Jack's shoulder. "Speaking of the Wicked Duke, is that Tavistock?"

The air in Jack's lungs escaped in a whoosh as he spun about and searched wildly for the man in question. There he was on the pavement, contemplating the entrance to the club, a diminutive figure in his typical overlarge costume.

Pennington was already on his way toward Tavistock before Jack could halt him. And what could he say anyway? He ended up muttering, "Bloody hell," as he followed Pennington.

"Tavistock," Pennington said, "I didn't know you were coming here. We could have shared a hack."

Tavistock nodded vaguely. "It was a spontaneous decision. I thought I'd come and see what I could find out about what you said earlier."

"Indeed?" Pennington stroked his chin. "Let us go inside. We'll have some brandy and poke around." He grinned at Tavistock, and Jack didn't like it one bit. What had Pennington said that had lured Tavistock to Brooks's where Tavistock was most certainly *not* a member?

Jack gave Pennington a smooth smile, then turned a hardened gaze on the younger *man*. "As it happens, I need to speak with Tavistock privately."

"Ah, well. I'll just go in, then." Pennington looked toward Tavistock. "Find me when you're finished. Mayhap I'll have news for you." His lips spread in an eager grin before he took himself into the club.

Tavistock didn't quite meet Jack's eyes. "Why do you need to speak with me?"

"Walk with me." Jack pivoted, anxious to usher Tavistock away from the entrance. "I was just on my way to the Wicked Duke. We can share a hack."

"As I said, I've only just arrived, so I won't be leaving yet." Tavistock's tone was affable. "You heard Pennington. We have plans for a drink."

Jack stepped toward Tavistock and lowered his voice to a mere whisper. "If you go inside, it's likely someone will realize you are not a member."

"How do you know I'm not a member?" Color rose in Tavistock's cheeks above his dark brown whiskers. They were truly the most ridiculous things, only slightly worse than his wiry brown wig.

"Because last time I checked, Brooks's didn't extend membership to women."

All the color above Lady Viola Fairfax's faux facial hair drained until she was the color of alabaster.

"Shall we go?" He nearly offered her his arm. Wouldn't that have set the tongues wagging!

She pressed her mouth into a firm line and glanced toward the door. Her hesitation was maddening. "You can't go in. If you're found out…" He shook his head briskly. "Does Eastleigh know you're here?"

"That's none of your concern." She managed to keep her Tavistock voice in place, even in a whisper, and for that, he gave her credit.

"Then I'll just ask him." He'd known Eastleigh since Oxford and considered him a good friend.

She blanched again. "Please don't. I'll go." She muttered an oath.

"You've quite mastered this act," he said.

She arched a brow at him. "Apparently, I haven't." Then she stalked past him, and he had to practically dash after her to keep up.

"I'll escort you home," he offered.

"That won't be necessary." She still spoke as Tavistock, her voice low and gravelly. Suddenly stopping, she turned to face him. "How did you know, and for how long?"

Jack had seen Tavistock—*her*—bend over once. The curve of a feminine backside had been absolutely unmistakable. Put together with her lush bow-shaped lips and the sparkle of her cerulean eyes framed with impossibly long lashes, her womanhood had been starkly apparent. At least to him. "Suffice it to say, you inadvertently displayed a part of your anatomy that left your sex completely discernible. That was well over a year ago. I don't remember when specifically."

She blinked at him. "My…anatomy?"

He coughed. "Your backside. To be specific."

She reached down and tugged at the tails of her coat as if she were trying to ensure they covered her sufficiently.

"You'd bent over," he clarified. "Also, I'm observant."

"Does anyone else know?"

"Not that I'm aware of. I certainly didn't tell anyone."

"And yet you'd tell my brother now?" There was a sardonic edge to the question.

"Doesn't he know?" Jack could have sworn he did. Once Jack had discerned her identity, he noticed they talked quietly from time to time. If one looked very closely, one would see the similarity in their chins.

"Yes, he knows. But not that I came here." She narrowed her eyes at him. "You won't really tell him, will you?"

"No, but I probably should. He's one of my closest friends." When she opened her mouth, presumably to protest, he said, "However, I am not going to, because you're going to allow me to escort you home. Where is that?"

"Berkeley Square." She'd finally given up the pretense of Tavistock's lower register.

Jack hailed a hack and gave the direction to the driver while she climbed into the vehicle. He followed her inside, sitting opposite her on the rear-facing seat.

She cast her head back against the squab and crossed her arms. "Are you sure no one else knows?"

"No, I'm *not* sure. As I said, I've never discussed it with anyone." What would he have said, *Did you know Tavistock is really the Duke of Eastleigh's sister?* He nearly laughed at the thought before soberly continuing, "I can't imagine Pennington knew. He was eager to drink brandy with you inside the club. How did you plan to get in anyway?"

She took a couple of breaths, and a smile teased her mouth. When she did that, it was impossible not to see a woman. An attractive woman. Ridiculous sideburns and all. "I was waiting for a group to enter and planned to just slip inside along with them."

"That might have worked." He was impressed

with her forethought, but then her deception clearly took considerable planning and effort. "Or, you may have been immediately discovered and tossed out for not being a member or someone's guest."

"Good to know. Next time, I'll say I'm *your* guest."

Not just a believable gentleman, she was also a brazen minx. "You can't mean to plan to try again?"

"I can and I do. I'm a journalist, and Pennington alerted me to a story I must follow."

Jack recalled what she'd said earlier. "What did Pennington tell you?"

After a brief hesitation, she told him. "Earlier at the Wicked Duke, he mentioned a rumor about an MP who has aligned himself with the radicals."

Jack made a sound of disgust low in his throat. "Don't pay attention to rumors, especially stupid ones like that. There are a number of MPs who are at least sympathetic to the radicals' concerns—myself included."

"True, but have any of them provided outright assistance?"

Jack leaned slightly forward, his interest piqued. "What kind of assistance?"

She angled her head and elevated her chin. "I don't know yet. Unfortunately, you interrupted my investigation."

"Your…" Jack shook his head. "You can't mean to conduct an actual investigation." But she did. She'd said as much.

She recrossed her arms and her brows, which she'd darkened to match her faux hair, pitched low over her indignant eyes. "Why, because I'm a woman?"

"I didn't say that, but yes, in part."

"You're no better than those ninnyhammers at the *Ladies' Gazette*."

He blinked at her. "Don't you write for the *Ladies' Gazette?*"

"As S. D. Tavistock. They had no interest in hiring *Viola* to write for them." She threw her hands up and lifted her voice in mock horror. "Heaven forfend a woman actually write for a woman's magazine!"

"I'm not saying you shouldn't investigate but that it will be difficult for you." When she opened her mouth, he added, "Yes, as a woman."

Her jaw clenched. "You are, sadly, correct. It will be difficult, which is why you deterring me from Brooks's tonight was so very frustrating."

"I stand by what I did."

"That's not surprising. You're a typical man who thinks he can order a woman about. However, I'm not your family, and I'm certainly not your wife."

"No, thank goodness. I've no need of one of those."

"I've even less need of a husband." She turned her head toward the window as they approached Berkeley Square.

He softened his tone. "It was never my intent to order you about. I was trying to prevent a catastrophe."

"I am trying to appreciate your concern."

Jack heard the disappointment in her voice and considered her perspective, how bloody hard it must be to be told you can't do things because you're a woman. "How about I help you with your investigation?"

She glanced over at him from the side of her eye. "Why?"

"Because I could ensure you're safe and help you gain access to...places." He wasn't sure he wanted to take her to Brooks's, even as his guest, but perhaps he'd consider it.

She gave him an arch look. "Or maybe you want to find out who this MP is."

Definitely. "I must admit to being curious. However, you should consider it's probably not even true."

The coach pulled into Berkeley Square and stopped near the curb. She reached for the door at the same moment Jack did. His hand covered hers, and they both pulled back as if the door handle had been on fire.

Their gazes connected for a brief moment, and Jack felt the same imagined heat as the not-blistering door handle. "Where is your house?" he asked, staring out the window to avoid looking at her.

"In the middle on this side. I didn't give the number because I don't like to get out in front. I go in through the mews so I can change before I go inside."

"The dowager is not aware of your masquerade?" Jack had met her grandmother, the formidable Dowager Duchess of Eastleigh, on a few occasions.

"Absolutely not, and she never will."

The door to the hack opened, and the driver stood outside.

Lady Viola jumped down. Jack followed her and paid the driver before she could.

She pursed her lips at Jack as the driver climbed back onto the hack. "You didn't need to do that."

"I don't need to walk you home either, but I'm going to. On second thought, I do need to walk you home."

The hack pulled away, and she stood beneath the street lantern with a perturbed expression. "I've done so countless times without your supervision."

"Obviously, but if this is the one night you encountered difficulty and I'd abandoned you, I'd never forgive myself. Neither would Eastleigh."

"Val will not know we were together, not unless

you tell him." She sent him a wary look. "You said you weren't going to tell him."

"I won't." He regarded her a moment. "You're a bit thorny this evening."

"And you're overbearing."

He supposed he was. Taking a deep breath and slowly expelling it, he summoned a placid smile. "Let us have a truce. I should very much like to help you determine whether an MP has aided the radicals in some way. May I do that?"

"Since you've asked very nicely, and I suspect your assistance may prove beneficial, I will accept your offer." She flashed him a brief smile before growing serious once more. "I require your solemn pledge that you will inform me of anything you hear and will not try to stop me from publishing my findings."

"Is that why you're doing this?"

"Yes. As I said, I'm a journalist in search of the truth. I want to write something more than 'observations from a gentleman.'"

Jack couldn't stop the short laugh that escaped him. "A gentleman who isn't really a gentleman."

She surprised him with a grin, and once again, he saw the radiant woman beneath the disguise. Then she pivoted and walked to the mews that ran along the backs of the houses. At the entrance to the mews, she stopped and faced him. "This is as far as you can come. I don't want to be seen arriving with you."

"Then someone knows you are Tavistock?"

"Yes, the head coachman and my maid keep my secret. Aside from Val and his wife and Val's partner, Colehaven, they are the only ones who know. And you, apparently."

"I will keep your secret until—and if—a time arises when I cannot for your own safety."

"That is fair. I should like to continue my investigation tomorrow evening. Can you meet me at the Wicked Duke? We can devise a strategy and leave from there."

"I can't tomorrow night. Can we go the night after?"

"I'll see you then." She turned and walked away.

"I'll look forward to it," he called after her.

Would he really? He didn't particularly have time to oversee a zealous journalist. And yet, he was eager to find out if there was any truth to this rumor she'd heard.

As he walked back to the street in search of a hack, he considered what she'd said about publishing her findings. Would the *Ladies' Gazette* publish something political, something that even mentioned radicals?

It was an anxious time with the Seditious Meetings Act and the Committee of Secrecy, not to mention the attack on the Prince Regent. Many of Jack's colleagues were fearful, and others were outraged.

Jack hailed a hack and was soon on his way to the Wicked Duke. He'd toss back an ale and see what he could learn. Hopefully, Eastleigh wouldn't be there. Jack felt uncomfortable not telling him about Lady Viola, but he'd made a deal with her, and he was a man of his word.

He leaned his head back against the squab. Seeing her at Brooks's had been a shock. She was incredibly foolish, but also, he had to admit, clever.

If she was a fool for sneaking into Brooks's, what was he for offering to help her?

CHAPTER 3

"*I*'m pleased you decided to come with me this evening," Grandmama said as the coach arrived at the Poole town house.

"It's just a soirée," Viola said with a touch of surprise. "Pleased" was a positively effusive expression from the dowager, who was as austere and detached as a person could be. On the outside, anyway. On the inside was a woman who adored her grandchildren and put family above everything. One need only look at the way she'd welcomed Isabelle into their fold when she'd wed Val several weeks ago.

Grandmama narrowed her eyes. "It's not *just* a soirée, my dear. It's an opportunity for you to consider reentering the Marriage Mart."

Panic rose in Viola's chest. Did she really mean to bring this up now? "Grandmama, I am not fit for the Marriage Mart."

"Bah, that was five years ago. An ancient scandal. You are invited nearly everywhere now."

Because she was the granddaughter of the ferocious Dowager Duchess of Eastleigh. If not for their relation, Viola would be an absolute pariah. As it was, she was at least a minor pariah.

The door to the coach opened, preventing further discussion. For now. Viola felt certain her grandmother would continue her campaign, both in public and private. She would be direct in private, but in public, she would ensure Viola met certain gentlemen or was seen in a particular light. Oh, this was a disaster. She had to convince Grandmama that she couldn't marry.

She *wouldn't* marry.

Val would help her. Probably. Maybe. After years of suffering Grandmama's sole focus regarding marriage, he would surely be sympathetic. Or perhaps he'd simply shrug and say it was Viola's turn.

No, he wouldn't do that. He understood why she'd called off her wedding even though the church had filled with guests. Furthermore, he'd supported her then just as he did now.

As they approached the front door of the town house, Grandmama murmured, "Don't forget what I said. There will be single gentlemen in attendance."

She'd timed the comment perfectly, because Viola didn't have time to respond before the butler greeted them and welcomed them inside. They gave their wraps to a footman and went upstairs to the drawing room.

Tables arranged with newspapers, caricatures, and natural objects Mr. Poole had brought back from a recent visit to the outer islands of Scotland were scattered about the room. Viola spotted rocks and shells and even a glass bottle filled with sand. She'd decided to come to this soirée because it was to be a conversation party, meaning there would be a great deal of conversation, *plus* Poole had many friends in the House of Commons. Viola hoped she might hear something about the mystery MP who might have assisted the radicals.

"Find me a seat, if you will," Grandmama said, drawing Viola's attention from the tables.

"Of course." Viola escorted her to a table near the center of the room, where she could see and be seen. "Will this do?"

Grandmama sank into the chair and arranged her skirt to drape attractively about her legs and feet. "Quite, thank you." Her gaze went to the door. "Oh, here are Eastleigh and Isabelle."

Viola turned to see her brother and sister-in-law coming toward them. Now she was doubly glad she'd come.

"Good evening," Val said with a touch of surprise. "I didn't realize you would be here." Because more often than not, Viola didn't accompany their grand-mother out.

Viola shrugged. "You know I like a good conver-sation party."

He arched a brow, indicating he perhaps didn't know that at all, but said nothing.

"I'm especially glad you're here," Isabelle said, lowering her voice to add, "I'm still a trifle nervous."

A former governess, Isabelle had been hesitant to become a duchess, but true love had won out, and now she was one of the most sought-after guests in town. When she attended a ball or a rout, the hostess was instantly celebrated. It was, to Viola and to Is-abelle, absurd.

"Don't be," Grandmama responded. "You are the toast of London this Season. You and Lady Penelope. Has she settled on a match yet?"

Viola and Isabel blinked at each other. As if either one of them would know. Viola *should* know since she made a career of writing gossip, but she focused on gentlemen. As far as she was aware, no one had made an offer. "Nothing I've heard about," Viola said. "Perhaps she'll be here tonight since there will apparently be a stock of eligible bachelors." She didn't bother hiding the sarcasm from her tone.

Grandmama said nothing but shot Viola a vexed glance before turning her attention to Val. "How is the circulating library coming?"

He smiled at his wife. "You'll have to ask Isabelle, as it is entirely her endeavor."

"Not entirely," Isabelle said with a light laugh. "You've plenty of opinions on which books we should stock."

He nodded. "This is true, and it is quite difficult not to buy them all."

Viola was so glad to see her brother happy. He'd been in love with Isabelle—secretly—for a decade, and Viola was glad that her brother was one of the lucky few to find a person with whom he could be entirely himself. It was much harder for women, and not just because they outnumbered the men due to the war. Isabelle, however, had landed one of the good ones.

They chatted for a few more minutes before Val went to speak with another gentleman and Grandmama's dearest friend, Lady Dunwich, arrived. Once she was seated next to Grandmama, Viola felt as though she could step away and meander among the tables. Isabelle joined her.

"So these rocks and shells are from," Isabelle leaned toward the table to read the card, "Arran. And we're to discuss them?"

"Yes, they're to spark conversation. As are the newspapers and caricatures."

Isabelle inclined her head toward the caricature on the table featuring two women in outlandish hats. "I'm not sure what to say about that other than have you ever seen a hat like that?"

"Of course not. Hats like that don't actually exist. And neither do women who look like that." One was very tall and excessively thin, while the other was squat and impossibly round.

"This is supposed to prompt meaningful discourse?" Isabelle shook her head. "They should have placed books on the tables. Those are *real* conversation starters."

Viola nodded enthusiastically. "I couldn't agree more." She glanced toward her grandmother to check on her as she often did when they were out together. Two gentlemen stood speaking with her and her friend. Grandmama's gaze drifted toward Viola, and the gentlemen followed it.

"Blast," Viola breathed.

"What's wrong?" Isabelle asked with concern.

"Grandmama has decided it's time I consider marriage. It looks as though she's trying to draw attention—male attention—to me." She groaned softly and turned her back to the group.

Isabelle linked her arm through Viola's and escorted her to a far corner of the room. "Allow me to save you."

Viola laughed. "Just when I think it's impossible to like you more than I already do, you prove me wrong. Thank you."

"I hope you don't mind my asking, but why come tonight if you knew she meant to play matchmaker?"

"I didn't know until we arrived. Ironically I *hadn't* planned to come; however, I decided I wanted to see if I might hear something that would be worth including in my column." Viola had told Isabelle about her hidden identity, and not just because she knew she couldn't expect Val to keep secrets from his wife. That had been a big part of it, but it was also nice to have a friend with whom she could discuss her work.

"That makes sense," Isabelle said. "Though how will you say you heard it here since Tavistock is not in attendance?"

"In these instances, I say, 'I have it from a dear friend who was there...' but I never name the friend."

"Extraordinary that you're able to do that." Isabelle shook her head, a slight smile playing about her mouth. "I couldn't even manage to pass myself off as a gentleman for a single evening." She'd tried once at Viola's behest. Viola had been trying to play matchmaker between her and Val. It had, much to her delight, worked.

"Mastering the act of playing a gentleman took plenty of practice. I spent many days in the park as Tavistock before I worked up the courage to go to the Wicked Duke."

"Well, you make it look easy," Isabelle said. "And you're quite successful. Two years and no one's discovered your identity or even realized you aren't a man."

That wasn't true, of course. As if conjured by their conversation, Jack Barrett strode into the drawing room. Viola's breath caught—because she was surprised to see him, particularly since he'd just come to her mind. It wasn't because of how he looked with his jet-black hair waving back from his intensely handsome features. Ebony brows arched above his walnut-brown eyes and his strong cheekbones slashed down toward the dimples that, when he laughed, creased around his mouth.

But he wasn't laughing now. He was intently searching the room, and then his gaze settled on her. It was as if he'd found what he was looking for.

Their eyes locked, and a flash of heat swept over her. The moment was over almost as soon as it had begun when he pivoted and walked in another direction. Unsurprisingly, he hadn't been looking for her. He had no reason to seek out Lady Viola Fairfax.

"Oh look, there's Diana. Let's go and speak with her." Isabelle started toward their friend, the Duchess of Colehaven. She and Isabelle had become rather close over the past few weeks. Since they were both newly married and to men who were best friends, they were well on their way to becoming best friends themselves.

All during their conversation, Viola's gaze kept straying to Mr. Barrett, who stood with a few other gentlemen near the table with the bottle of sand. Garbed in a perfectly tailored black coat with black breeches and a midnight-blue waistcoat, he presented an intimidating and alluring figure. She couldn't seem to stop glancing in his direction.

He didn't appear to be aware of her presence, not after looking right at her and walking away. Was he purposely ignoring her? It was probably for the best. And yet, she was vaguely annoyed.

"Pardon me," she murmured before making her way slowly to the table next to the one where Mr. Barrett stood. She picked up a shell and held it to her ear.

"Do you hear the ocean?"

She turned her head to see Mr. Barrett had moved next to her. Not that she'd needed to turn to see who it was—she recognized the deep, seductive timbre of his voice.

Seductive?

"Yes." She handed him the shell.

He put it to his ear, and a half smile tilted his lips. Viola's chest tightened in reaction. "It's magic," he said before replacing the shell on the table.

"It's actually the noise from the room gathering in the shell and bouncing back to your ear." Why had she said that? Magic sounded rather charming.

He chuckled. "I know what it is. But I like to think it's the ocean. I haven't been there in some time."

"I haven't either."

"I love its vastness and the never-ending rush of

waves over the shore. It makes me think of how complicated and yet simple our world can be."

"That's rather contradictory," she said, picking up a rock that had been smoothed by the waves he spoke of.

"Life is full of contradictions, wouldn't you say, *Lady* Viola?" He was referring to her disguise as Tavistock. She suppressed the urge to smile.

"It can be, yes. So this is why you couldn't meet tonight?" she asked quietly.

"Yes. And it seems you weren't available either."

She put the rock back down and moved around the table so they could put some distance between themselves and other guests. "I hadn't planned to come tonight, but then decided it was worth trying to learn anything I could about our…project."

He nodded twice, slowly. "Yes, our project. We should perhaps develop a strategy for tomorrow night. I will ensure Pennington will be there."

"Excellent, I do think he is our best hope for delving deeper into things. We need to find out how he heard this rumor."

"Agreed. He typically likes to talk, so it shouldn't be too difficult."

Viola didn't disagree, but she wouldn't leave things to chance alone. "And if he's being close-mouthed, we'll pour ale down his throat until he speaks."

Mr. Barrett's dark eyes widened very briefly. "You wish to get him drunk?" He kept his voice low.

Viola lifted a shoulder. "If we must."

"Diabolical," he said. "I like it. Tell me, Lady Viola, have you ever been drunk? It seems as though you must have, given your frequent visits to the Wicked Duke."

"I am careful not to overimbibe. Indeed, I rarely

finish an entire mug of Colehaven's marvelous ale." She shook her head with regret. "It's a crime."

He laughed. "Indeed."

"To answer your question, yes. I have been drunk." She narrowed her eyes at him, but not in anger or disgust. "That is not a question you should ask a lady."

"I'm sorry," he whispered. "I should have said, 'Tell me, Tavistock, have you ever been drunk?'" His eyes glowed with mirth, and she felt herself responding to his good humor.

She angled her head to a saucy tilt. "No."

"So you've been drunk as Lady Viola, not as Tavistock." He studied her intently, and her toes had the audacity to curl in her slippers. "Fascinating."

"Only once—just to see what it was like."

"You are a woman dedicated to investigation, it seems."

She was more than impressed with his estimation. She was...flattered. "That is an excellent way to describe me." She tried to think of how she would describe him and wasn't sure. Not yet. But they'd be spending plenty of time together, probably. Unless they unraveled the entire mystery tomorrow night.

She realized she didn't particularly want to. It might be fun to be on the hunt with Mr. Barrett.

No, that was madness. He was not her friend—or anything else—just a necessary partner who shared her objective of learning the truth.

"So, we'll move forward with our operation tomorrow evening," Mr. Barrett said. "We have meetings at Westminster tomorrow, and I'll bring Pennington when they conclude."

"I'll be waiting." Eagerly. Because of the investigation, and only because of the investigation.

"See you then." He inclined his head and turned from her. As he walked away, she saw Grandmama staring in her direction. The dowager notched her chin in the way that meant, *Do come here*.

Viola steeled herself to hear about the bachelors in attendance. Meanwhile, she'd think about talking to Pennington tomorrow and not how much she was looking forward to seeing Jack Barrett again.

CHAPTER 4

"*D*on't you think Falworth is being unreasonable?" Jack asked, still angry about the encounter he and Pennington had just had at Westminster.

They alighted from the hack in front of the Wicked Duke, Pennington stepping down first and Jack following. "I don't know if he's being *unreasonable*," Pennington said. "He's entitled to his opinion, and he doesn't see a problem with our current voting laws."

"Bah," Jack grumbled as they walked into the tavern.

A loud refrain of "Barrett! Pennington!" greeted them, and Jack relaxed. Walking into the Wicked Duke always felt somewhat like coming home. It was familiar and comfortable, though it lacked his father, whom he was overdue to visit. It had been too long, particularly since he only lived in Isleworth, a mere ten miles away.

"What news today, gentlemen?" This came from Lady Viola—Jack wasn't sure he could ever think of the "man" as Tavistock now—who sat at a table near the front window.

Seeing her as a man again was jarring, particularly

after how lovely she'd looked last night. She was a beautiful woman, with golden-blonde hair, vivid blue eyes, and a face that could never be mistaken for masculine. And yet she managed to fool everyone with the addition of fake sideburns. It was more than that, he realized as he scrutinized her now. She held her mouth differently, somehow diminishing the lush bow shape of her lips. She was also careful to hood her eyes, letting her lids droop much of the time. It was an astonishing transformation and undoubtedly required impressive discipline.

"Tavistock, weren't you just here the other night?" Pennington asked as he moved toward her table. "Don't typically see you twice in the same week."

Lady Viola shrugged as she lifted her mug. "I enjoy the Wicked Duke as much as the next man."

Next man. Jack suddenly felt as if he were in on a private joke, and he supposed he was. Only it wasn't a joke to her. She had adopted the Tavistock persona for very specific reasons. Reasons that required she wasn't Lady Viola. It was a crime she had to pretend to be someone she wasn't in order to write for the *Ladies' Gazette.*

Mary, one of the barmaids, met them at Lady Viola's table with two mugs of ale. "I brought you the porter," she said to Jack. "I know that's your preference when it's available." She winked at him before turning away.

"What news today?" Lady Viola repeated, her gaze fixed on Pennington, who was taking a long draught of ale.

"I was just trying to calm Barrett down," Pennington said, tossing a grin at Jack. "He's easily agitated these days."

"Anyone with an ounce of care should be," Jack muttered before sipping the porter, which was absolutely delightful and precisely what he needed.

"There is no shortness of agitation, to be sure," Lady Viola said diplomatically.

"Indeed. Bloody well drove Cobbett right out of the country!" Pennington arched his brows as he lifted his mug for another drink.

The mention of William Cobbett sparked Jack's concern. He peered across the table at Lady Viola. Cobbett published a radical-leaning newspaper that was popular with the working class and had felt the need to travel to America before he was arrested for sedition. Since he'd already spent time in prison for libel a few years back, he'd likely made a sensible decision.

Jack could only hope that Lady Viola also proved to be sensible. He'd have to make certain of it. She was right that there was no shortness of agitation right now, and it would be far too easy to find trouble.

Pennington leaned over the table and looked from Lady Viola to Jack, then back to Lady Viola again. When he spoke, it was in a low, furtive tone. "Just look at that march from Manchester. Workers are angry, and they want to be heard."

"And yet we've taken away their ability to meet and organize a way to be heard," Jack said sardonically, which earned him a sharp look from Pennington.

"Careful what you say, Barrett." Pennington leaned back. "Not with me, of course," he added jovially. "You may say what you like, and I shan't repeat it."

Jack swallowed an answering snort. The entire reason they were here tonight was to coax Pennington to spread gossip more than he already had. But he was right about one thing: Jack had to be careful what he said. He was far more radically minded than he let on, and sometimes he let on far too much.

"Sir Humphrey! Caldwell!"

Jack didn't join his tablemates and everyone else in the main salon in welcoming the two newest arrivals. Instead, he busied himself pouring porter down his throat. Sir Humphrey and Caldwell were two of his chief opponents when it came to reforming Parliament. They represented boroughs that didn't need representation—at least not at the current level. Why should Caldwell's borough have two MPs for seven bloody voters when other boroughs had two MPs for thousands?

Naturally, Sir Humphrey and Caldwell sat down at their table. Jack stifled a groan and this time drained his tankard. Hell, he was supposed to be getting Pennington drunk, not himself.

When Mary brought ale for Sir Humphrey and Caldwell, he asked her to bring a round of brandy for everyone. His gaze met Lady Viola's, and she nodded imperceptibly.

"That's mighty generous of you, Barrett," Pennington said.

"Seems like we might need it after today."

Sir Humphrey lifted his mug. "I would agree with that, and I'll add my thanks."

Pennington frowned and shook his head. "We were just discussing the state of things. Such a mess right now." He looked over at Lady Viola and put his hand on her shoulder. "Be glad you aren't an MP."

Jack froze as he stared at the man touching her. Would he realize? Beyond that concern, Jack had to suppress the urge to smack Pennington's hand away for daring to touch her.

Lady Viola reached for her mug with the arm extending from the shoulder Pennington clasped, neatly evicting his grasp. "Exceedingly glad, thank you."

Pennington winced, then looked over Sir Humphrey, Caldwell, and Jack. "I haven't just reminded you that you're on opposite sides of several issues, have I?"

"You have now," Sir Humphrey cracked.

Jack lifted his empty mug in a silent toast but couldn't drink. Thankfully, the brandy arrived. He was careful to take just a sip. He needed to focus on Pennington. He just wished Sir Humphrey and Caldwell hadn't come.

Caldwell's thin lips spread in a questionable smile. "Just because we don't always agree doesn't mean we can't enjoy a drink at our favorite gathering place. Isn't that right, Barrett?"

"Quite."

"Still, you must admit Barrett has a point with regard to rotten boroughs," Pennington continued, illustrating he was truly one of the most obtuse men in Parliament. While *he* wasn't from a rotten borough, Sir Humphrey and Caldwell were.

"Let's not discuss it." Caldwell's tone held a bit of an edge.

"You represent Gatton in Surrey, do you not?" Lady Viola asked. "And they have, what, seven voters in total?" She looked to Sir Humphrey. "And you represent Bramber in Sussex, with perhaps twenty voters?"

Sir Humphrey shifted uncomfortably, as he typically did when the subject arose. It clearly bothered him, but not enough to change anything. He was quite happy in his comfortable seat, which was handed to him at every election by the Marquess of Bramber.

Caldwell looked at her intently. "You aren't writing about such matters, are you?"

Warning bells signaled in Jack's mind. This was not a safe path of conversation.

"Just informing myself," Lady Viola said with a tight smile. "I have no opinion on the subject. My job is to deliver information."

Jack gave her a pointed stare. "Surely the readers of the *Ladies' Gazette* have no interest in such things."

"They do not appear to."

Jack thought he heard the defeat in her voice. She wanted to write something important that people cared about—or what they *should* care about.

"Then perhaps we should turn the conversation to what they do care about," Sir Humphrey offered with a grin before sipping his brandy. "What do the readers of the *Ladies' Gazette* want to know?"

"They like to know what happens inside places like these. I shall report upon the drinks that were imbibed and the amusements that were enjoyed." She looked at each of them in turn. "What do you do to amuse yourselves?"

Sir Humphrey gave his head a rueful shake. "Billiards. Can't seem to get enough of it."

"Then let's go play," Lady Viola suggested. She stood and picked up her mug.

Quickly finishing his brandy, his face pinching as he swallowed and set the empty glass on the table, Sir Humphrey rose with his ale. "Let's."

"I'll come along." Caldwell got to his feet and inclined his head at Jack as he picked up his beer and the brandy. "Barrett."

"Caldwell," Jack said, also inclining his head in the way that men did when they acknowledged an opponent.

As the trio set off, Lady Viola slid him a wide-eyed glance and inclined her head slightly toward Pennington. She seemed to be indicating she was giving him the opportunity to get the information they needed without Sir Humphrey and Caldwell about. She was, as he'd already assessed, quite clever.

Jack also noted that she'd left her brandy. Good, he'd make sure Pennington drank it. Over the next half hour, they spoke of horses and racing, their gazes drifting toward perhaps the best whip in the city, Giles Langford, seated on the other side of the salon. When Pennington finished his brandy, Jack suggested he take Tavistock's.

"He might come back for it," Pennington argued.

"Then I'll buy him another. Drink it," Jack urged with a chuckle.

"He's an odd fellow, isn't he?" Pennington mused as he lifted the glass for a sip. "I used to wonder where he was when he wasn't here. I never saw him anywhere else until the other night at Brooks's. Had no idea he was a member."

"I think he's a member at Boodle's too," Jack said vaguely. "I'm sure I've seen him there."

He told the lie easily and would tell her about it. He would also tell her she needed to be careful. If someone as dim-witted as Pennington noticed her behavior, a sharper mind, such as Caldwell's, would perhaps realize much more. If they took the time to think about it. Hopefully, they wouldn't.

Jack began to see why she kept her visits infrequent—the old adage "out of sight, out of mind" seemed to fit her situation perfectly. He'd encourage her to adhere to that.

"Ah, I'll have to keep an eye out. He's a pleasant fellow, though he never did join me inside Brooks's the other night." Pennington frowned. "I thought we were going to have a drink."

"That was my fault, I'm afraid." Jack sipped his brandy. "We got to talking and then we left. Went to a gaming hell." He'd no idea why he added that detail, but reasoned it could only help Lady Viola's act. "Sh

—" Hell, he'd almost said she! "Should have told you, but forgot. He did mention later that he was supposed to talk with you, something about a rumor about an MP."

Pennington nodded as he took another drink of brandy. "Ghastly rumor. I probably shouldn't have repeated it."

Jack swung his head and upper body toward Pennington. "What was it again?"

"Bah, I shouldn't say. As I said, I probably shouldn't have said anything in the first place."

Jack wasn't going to give up so easily. "I remember now, an MP actually helped the radicals with something. Which radicals, I wonder? The Spencean Philanthropists? The Hampdens?"

"That, I don't know."

"Ah, well, rumors do make things more interesting, don't they?" Jack overrode his frustration with a forced laugh and tapped his brandy glass to Pennington's. The other man obliged, lifting the glass that had been meant for Lady Viola and draining it.

Jack glanced about and lowered his voice. "Did you hear it here? Perhaps we should be careful what we say."

"Not here, no. The Wicked Duke is safe territory for all!" Pennington shook his head vigorously. "No, I heard it at that coffeehouse on St. James's. That's the best place to hear rumors. If you want to, that isss." Pennington had begun to slur.

Jack pounced. "Yes, it seems quite a few MPs like to frequent that establishment." Jack had spent some time there in his younger days, when he'd been a barrister, before he'd become an MP, following in his father's footsteps to the letter. "Did you hear this rumor from an MP, or was it one of the employees?"

"Neither." Pennington waggled his brows, then leaned close, exhaling his brandy-ale breath over

Jack's face. "It was that solicitor who always sits at the corner table. Hodges."

Triumph surged in Jack's veins. He was more than familiar with Hodges; the man had once worked for Jack's father. That had been decades ago, but he would know Jack, and there was no reason to expect he wouldn't share the same information he'd given Pennington. Hopefully, he'd share even more. Jack just hoped he *knew* more. If he didn't, perhaps he could point Jack and Lady Viola in the right direction.

Lady Viola. All this time, she'd been holding her own with the annoying Sir Humphrey and Caldwell. Jack leapt to his feet. "I've a sudden urge to play billiards as well." He looked at Pennington in question but stopped short of inviting him.

Pennington waved his hand before letting it drop to the table, his palm loudly smacking the wood. "You go. I've a need for another ale, methinksss."

He probably didn't, but Jack wouldn't stand in his way. He moved into the billiard room and saw that Lady Viola was watching him. Jack quickly made his way to her side and stopped dead.

One of her sideburns was barely hanging onto her face. He rushed forward and urgently whispered, "Your disguise is falling off."

Her hand came up to her cheek, and she felt the problem. Her eyes widened, and she started toward the door to the private salon, leaving the billiard room without a word.

Jack followed her out at a sedate pace. Once he got to the private salon, he saw her heading through a back doorway. He continued after her, ending up in a small, poorly lit storage room.

She turned as he entered, her breath drawn in a sharp gasp. Then her shoulders dipped in relief as she recognized it was him. She pushed the hair onto her face. "It won't stick."

He stepped forward and surveyed the problem. "No, it doesn't seem to want to."

"I have glue in my pocket, but I don't have a looking glass."

"Can I help?" he offered.

She reached into the pocket of her coat and pulled out a small jar. Opening the lid, she showed him that a brush was attached to the underside. "Just use this to dab the glue on." She set the lid back on and handed him the pot.

Jack took the brush and moved even closer. "Sorry," he murmured. "The light isn't very good in here. I'd hate to glue your mouth closed."

"My brother would probably appreciate that. At least he would have when we were younger." She laughed softly, completely abandoning the deeper tone of Tavistock's vocalizations. Her laugh was warm and alluring.

They were nearly chest to chest. "Can you tip your head back slightly?" he asked.

She did as he asked, and the lone lantern hanging on the wall splashed its meager light across her cheekbones. He swiped the brush into the glue. "A sparing amount?"

She started to nod but seemed to think better of it given his ministrations. "Yes."

He brushed the glue onto her face. "It's a shame you cover yourself up with these. Does it hurt when you take them off?"

"Not really," she said. "I'm quite used to it. Hold the hair in place for a moment so the glue will set."

Replacing the brush into the jar, he gently pressed the faux hair against her skin. It was an intimate caress, or it would have been if she were bare faced. Her gaze locked with his as his fingertips applied pressure. He was aware of the warmth of her flesh and a hint of fragrance that had no business belonging to a man. He hoped no one ever got this close to her and recalled how she'd expertly removed Pennington's hand earlier.

Jack's changed his mind. This *was* intimate. And only growing more so the longer they looked at each other and the longer he touched her face. He'd never been more aware of her as a woman.

"I think it's probably fine," she said softly.

As he withdrew his hand, he was struck by an image of her without the facial hair. Her lips were full—the top pointed in the middle and the bottom thick and lush—and he saw himself kissing them...

Jack took a long step back and thrust the pot toward her. "Back to normal."

Her hand closed around the jar, and he was careful not to touch her again lest the kissing idea take hold in his mind. She replaced the lid and stowed the glue away in her pocket. "You think this is normal? But you just said it's a shame I wear them."

"It is. I admit I much prefer you as Lady Viola, as you were last night. But this—Tavistock—is how I mostly know you."

She glanced away, and he wished he hadn't said all that. "Did you learn anything from Pennington?" Her gaze met his again, and anything that had sparked between them was gone, thank goodness.

He cleared his throat and shook out his shoulders, glad to be back on task. "Yes. Once I got him going on your brandy, he became rather loose-lipped. We need to see Mr. Hodges, a solicitor who sits at the corner table at the coffeehouse on St. James's."

Her eyes lit, and her mouth lifted. "Can you meet me there tomorrow?"

"I was going to suggest that very thing."

"Oh, good, I'm glad you're available. I'm not sure I would have had the patience to wait."

He frowned. "I expect that you would, however. We have an agreement."

She cocked her head to the side. "Are you still threatening to tell Val?"

"Maybe." He wasn't sure he would. He now felt a certain loyalty to her that he hadn't a few days ago. "Mostly, we are in this together, and I should hope that you would not go on without me."

She inclined her head. "I feel the same way. What time shall we meet?"

He mentally reviewed his appointments and meetings for the following day. "Two o'clock?"

"I'll be there."

He swept his gaze over her, trying to recall if she wore the same thing every time she assumed her masculine identity. "How many Tavistock costumes do you have?"

"Three. I just made a new waistcoat that I think is rather smart. You can tell me tomorrow if you agree."

"You make your own waistcoats?"

She gave him a droll look. "You think I have a tailor?"

He laughed then. At the absurdity of such a thing. At the absurdity of it all. "I'm leaving now. Can I see you home again?"

"Are you sure you want to? People might think we've become close friends like Sir Humphrey and Caldwell."

Jack shuddered. "Never say that. I should be horrified to be like either of them."

"You really don't care for them, do you?"

"They're part of the problem we have in this country right now. They're self-serving and corrupt. They don't give a fig about the Blanketeers who marched from Manchester or the thousands of other

people who don't feel as if their government repre-
sents them." He realized his voice had risen.

Her lips curved into a soft, very feminine smile.
"You are a true radical. Perhaps you should have accompanied Cobbett to America."

"Not a chance. I'm needed here."

"Yes, I daresay you are," she murmured. "Let us
depart." She moved past him out of the storage room.

As he followed her, he hoped they would learn
what they needed to at the coffeehouse tomorrow.
The sooner he stopped spending time with the
tempting Lady Viola, the better.

CHAPTER 5

*D*espite the new waistcoat, Viola resented her costume today. While she typically enjoyed the freedom masquerading as a man allowed her, today she found she was eager to be a woman. Not that she could be in this coffeehouse.

Stepping inside, she took in the counter on the opposite side of the large room, where a man brewed coffee. Tables with benches stood in lines, while other tables and benches were set against the walls with drapes between them to allow for privacy. At least she assumed that was the purpose of the drapes.

She was a few minutes early and didn't yet see Mr. Barrett. Her pulse quickened at the prospect of seeing him again. Was that why she wished she was dressed as a woman? He'd commented on liking it last night, and today she found she loathed the feel of the whiskers on her face. She couldn't help thinking how nice it might be if he flirted with her.

But would it be? She was being silly. And short-sighted. Her focus needed to be on uncovering this story, *not* on the devilishly handsome Jack Barrett.

Only he was more than handsome. He lived a life of purpose and seemed to genuinely care about those who were struggling. That was far more attractive to her than his looks. And that made him dangerous.

Pushing him from her thoughts, she scanned the interior of the coffeehouse. There were four corner tables. Which one was Hodges? Mr. Barrett hadn't described him, so Viola would just have to wait.

And yet, she didn't want to stand here and loiter. Two of the four corner tables were occupied. One held a trio of older men who were engaged in animated conversation, one of them gesturing wildly. The other table held a single man, perhaps in his late fifties, with a shock of white hair. His head was bent toward the newspaper spread in front of him across the table.

"Hodges, you need a refill?" the man at the bar called over to the single gentleman.

Hodges, apparently, looked up from his newspaper and flashed a smile. He pushed his spectacles up his nose. "Yes, please."

Viola strode toward his table. "I'll get it for you."

Blinking up at her from behind his glasses, Hodges inclined his head. "Why, thank you."

"My pleasure." Viola smiled, keeping her lips thin and closed, then picked up his cup and went to the counter.

"Put his on my account," Hodges called.

The coffee master refilled Hodges's cup and then filled another for Viola. She picked up both with a nod and returned to Hodges's table.

"I hope you'll sit with me," Hodges said as he folded the newspaper and set it to the side.

Viola glanced toward the door. She was supposed to wait for Jack, but he was now running late. Surely he would understand that she couldn't pass up this opportunity. "Thank you. I'm meeting someone."

Hodges smiled pleasantly. "He's welcome to join us when he arrives." He sipped his coffee and closed his eyes while he let out a satisfied sigh. "Nothing like a fresh cup."

While Viola had learned to like a variety of ales over the past two years, she hadn't ever tried coffee. She took a tentative sip of the dark, steaming brew and nearly sputtered. Forcing the sour liquid down her throat, she worked to hide her reaction.

However, she must not have been entirely successful, as Hodges chuckled. "It's a tad on the bitter side today."

"Yes," she agreed, setting the cup down. "I'm Tavistock, by the bye."

"Pleased to meet you. Name's Emory Hodges, solicitor by trade."

"I'm a writer," she said, removing her hat and setting it on the bench beside her.

Hodges tipped his head to the side and regarded her, his dark eyes contemplative behind his spectacles. "The Tavistock who writes the gentlemen's column for the *Ladies' Gazette?*"

Her jaw dipped in brief surprise before she snapped her mouth closed and blinked at him. "You read it?"

He chuckled again, and given the lines fanning from his eyes and the deep grooves on either side of his mouth, she gathered he did so often. "I read all sort of things. Can't be too informed. I pride myself on reading and learning as much as I can."

"An admirable endeavor," Viola said in earnest. "What were you reading today?" She glanced toward the newspaper.

He waved his hand at the *Times*. "Yet another article about the current disaster in the country, and how the radical workers must be kept in line lest they start another riot."

"You disagree?"

"I think it's dangerous to agitate people where

there is already plenty of discord. But people like to read that sort of thing—more and more, it seems."

"Yes. I find myself writing pieces to do with the current state of affairs."

One of Hodges's bushy white brows rose up above the edge of his glasses. "Not just who was seen where and what they were wearing?"

Viola tamped down her frustration—she didn't think he was looking down on her. "I am interested in political issues as they affect my readers."

"Yes, it affects us all, whether we pay attention or not. Well, you've come to the right place to hear about politics." He looked toward the opposite corner, where the three men were still enthusiastically conversing. "Just look at them. They're here every afternoon debating the same things over and over." He shook his head. "Retired MPs with nothing better to do." He leaned forward, his eyes twinkling. "Not that I have anything better to do! I like to come and keep my ears open. Still have excellent hearing." He tapped the side of his head as he sat back once more, his shoulders disturbing the drape.

Viola glanced toward the door. Jack was rather late now, and she wasn't sure there would be a better opening. She pinned Hodges with a shrewd stare. "Actually, I heard a rumor recently. Perhaps you know something about it. Involves an MP who helped the radicals with something."

The way Hodges's eyes lit and color infused his ruddy cheeks, Viola knew she'd found success. He leaned forward again, farther this time, and lowered his voice. Despite the decrease in volume, his excitement was evident. "Oh, I know precisely what you're speaking of. An MP instigated the attack on Prinny back in January."

Viola also pitched forward, her pulse thrumming. "Instigated? What do you mean?" They hadn't caught whoever had fired at his coach or thrown rocks or whatever they had done to break the window.

"Apparently, he organized it," Hodges said. "Told the radicals when to attack. They were ready and waiting when the prince left Westminster."

"So it wasn't just a random attack by disgruntled workers?" That was one theory Viola had heard.

Hodges shook his head slowly. "It seems it wasn't, but I'm not sure anyone knows for sure."

"You don't know who this MP is?" She held her breath, hoping he would.

"I'm afraid I don't, but if you find out, that'll be a story to print for sure!" He said this with such glee that Viola smiled as she imagined it. It would be incredible to publish this and could entirely change her career. Perhaps she could even write it under her real name. For a brief moment, she lost herself in the excitement of possibility.

"Are you going to include this in your column?" Hodges asked, sitting back. "I ask that you don't mention me. I don't want to be swept up in anything to do with anything radical." He shuddered. "Too easy to get thrown in prison right now for anything at all for who knows how long!"

He was absolutely right. It was as if he'd doused her in ice-cold water from the Thames. She nodded soberly. She could write this—as gossip—in her column, though she wasn't sure what her editor would say.

No, she couldn't do it. Hodges was right that it was dangerous, but that was because it was unsubstantiated. She needed proof. And she needed to discover the identity of the MP.

"I can't write this sort of gossip," she said with a twinge of regret. "It's a fascinating story—or it would be if I had more information, such as the identity of the MP. Is there anything else you could tell me that might lead me to him?"

He shook his head. "I can't even tell you who I heard it from, but it was here." He frowned and stared into his coffee cup for a moment. "I think." Shrugging, he sipped his coffee. "Can't say for sure."

Well, that wasn't helpful. Still, she now knew what the MP had done to help the radicals. And it was far more shocking than she'd imagined. To think that someone in Parliament had encouraged an attack on the Prince Regent was terrifying. "Makes me think of Spencer Perceval," she said softly, referring to the prime minister who'd been assassinated by an aggrieved merchant five years ago.

Hodges nodded sadly. "Hard not to draw a comparison. We must all be on our guard. Perhaps the newspaper articles *aren't* a bad thing." He glanced over at the newspaper on the table before looking back at her. "I hope you're able to find the truth. We deserve to know who would provoke such a thing. If he did it once, what might he do next?"

A shiver dashed down Viola's spine. "Indeed." She picked up her cup and took another tentative sip of the coffee. Though it had cooled, it was not any more palatable. She choked it down and decided that was all she could do. And where the devil was Barrett?

Swinging her head toward the door once more, she saw him enter. She didn't want to tell him about this in front of Hodges. "If you'll excuse me," she said, rising.

"Aren't you meeting someone?" he asked, looking up at her.

"Yes, he's just arrived, but we're off to another appointment. I do thank you for the company, and hope I'll see you soon."

"I'd like that," he said, smiling.

She swept up her hat and set it on her head before

pivoting and striding toward Barrett. His dark eyes flickered with recognition, then he frowned.

"Were you just sitting with Hodges?"

She nodded. "Let's go."

"But—"

"I'll tell you all about it outside." She moved past him and pushed open the door, stepping out into the gray sunlight. Thin, high clouds blocked the sun, but it was still bright. She pulled the brim of her hat lower as she started along St. James's.

Barrett fell into step beside her. "You were supposed to wait for me."

She shot him an apologetic glance. "I did try, but you were late. I had an opportunity to sit with Hodges, so I took it."

"I still say you should have waited." He pressed his lips together in dismay.

"Even though I learned what this MP did, and it's quite awful?"

Barrett stopped and moved closer to the corner of a building, away from the center of the pavement. "What did you learn?" His question was low and urgent, full of the anticipation she'd felt a short while ago.

"Hodges said this MP organized the attack on the Prince Regent."

Barrett drew in a sharp breath, his eyes narrowing with alarm. "That's madness."

"One would think."

"Who is it?"

"Hodges didn't know, unfortunately, but the man told the radicals where to be and when."

Barrett pivoted and leaned back against the stone, his shoulders dipping. "This MP could do it again."

"He could, but perhaps he sees the danger in it and won't."

"I should hope so. That event made an already

tense atmosphere even more strained. Look at all that's come of it—a secret committee, the suspension of habeas corpus, the resurrection of a Seditious Meetings Act. For someone trying to hinder the radicals, it worked rather well."

She could see that perspective as well as another. "Or maybe it was just someone who wanted to assassinate the prince."

"Well, they failed spectacularly at that, didn't they?" he said wryly. "Whatever their motive, they made a hell of an impact." He looked at her. "Pardon me. For a brief moment there, I forgot who you really are."

She'd thought that had become more difficult for him—not seeing her as a woman. To find it hadn't was disappointing, and she didn't want to think about why that was. "I'm Tavistock. At least for right now."

"You're bloody brilliant, that's for certain. I can't believe you managed to learn that from Hodges in less than thirty minutes."

"It was about thirty minutes. I think." She hadn't been watching the clock. Barrett's praise warmed her.

Barrett pushed away from the wall and started walking again. She moved alongside him.

"I'm sorry I was late. I was delayed at a meeting," he said. "I'm trying to think of who might have done this. Granted, I don't know every single MP, at least not closely, but that one of them would take this risk is very concerning."

"But not hard to believe, I imagine."

He slid her a glance as they walked. "What do you mean?"

"So many of them are corrupt—rotten boroughs, or they're serving in a seat that's been paid for by someone in the Lords," she said. "They'd have to feel beholden to behave in a certain way."

His mouth ticked up in a half smile that made her breath hitch. "You're quite clever. Yes, I shouldn't find this hard to believe. I suppose it's just that I don't *want* to believe it. I always hope people are better than what others might think them capable of, that we ultimately comport ourselves with decency and honor."

She could see that *he* did. His passion for his beliefs was evident. And inspiring. "I'd like to find out who this MP is—people deserve to know about this potential threat."

"In case he does it again, you mean." Barrett shook his head. "Yes, people deserve to know, just as they deserve proper representation so that they are heard. The way we allow people to vote—or not vote—is absolutely maddening." He spoke with considerable vitriol, and again his enthusiasm was palpable.

"I couldn't agree more. That women aren't allowed to vote or even own property, which would allow them to vote, is appalling. And yes, I realize a few women do, in fact, own property and vote, but they are by far a minority."

"So miniscule as to not even count," he said. "While I appreciate your zeal and do agree, I unfortunately think women's suffrage is a ways off yet." He winced as he apologized. "If we can get to universal male suffrage, that would be an important first step."

Logically, she understood the reality of what he was saying, but it was still frustrating. "I would argue we should move to universal suffrage period. Women have next to no rights at present, even fewer when they marry and give over what modicum of independence they might have to their husbands."

"Is that why you aren't married?" The question

was soft and uttered with more than a trace of curiosity. She could ignore it, but she didn't.

"Yes." They'd reached Piccadilly, and she stopped, intending to catch a hack. "And why aren't you married?"

His dark eyes glimmered beneath the brim of his hat. "Because I don't want to be. Not yet, anyway. I've too much to do right now."

She could see that. "You're married to the House of Commons."

He grinned. "Perhaps. Now, what is our next move?"

"To learn the identity of this MP so we can stop him from causing further harm."

"Agreed, but how to do this..." He pursed his lips as he gazed out at the busy thoroughfare. "I need to think on it. Will I see you at the Wicked Duke later?"

She shook her head. "I can't risk too many nights there."

"Then where else will you be?" He peered at her expectantly, and she could almost imagine he wanted her to be somewhere so he could see her socially. But that was preposterous. Neither of them were interested in such a connection.

"I'm not sure. I'll have to consult my grandmother's calendar." She hesitated a bare moment before saying, "I don't often go out with her. I don't particularly enjoy Society."

He nodded sharply. "Another thing we have in common. All right, then, I'll consider our next move —as will you. Why not send me a note as to where we can meet?"

"I'll do that."

She looked out at the street. "I just need a hack."

"Allow me." He hailed one, laughing as he shook his head. "I really have to stop thinking of you as a woman."

The disappointment she'd felt earlier evaporated in a wave of heat. She gave the driver her direction, then turned to Barrett. "Actually, I'd rather you didn't."

She didn't dare look at him again as she climbed into the vehicle. She also didn't dare think about what she'd just admitted out loud.

CHAPTER 6

*W*alking into the house in which Jack had grown up with his loving parents always felt like being wrapped in a warm hug. Tonight was no different as he handed his hat to his father's butler. "How are you, Michaelson?" Jack asked.

The tall Norseman inclined his still-blond head. "Quite well, thank you. Your father is delighted you've come for dinner tonight."

After thinking it had been too long since he'd visited, Jack had dispatched a note. "Please tell me Mrs. Fink has made lamb." Her recipe was Jack's favorite.

Michaelson's mouth lifted in a smile. "Of course."

Jack walked through the entrance hall into his father's library. The feeling of home intensified in this room, where he'd spent so much time with his father reading, learning, and just watching the man he admired most in the world.

His father looked up from his desk, his dark blue eyes peering at Jack over the tops of his half-moon glasses. "Jack, my boy." He took the spectacles off and set them atop the sheaf of papers he was reading, then stood. For a man nearing seventy, he didn't look a day over sixty, and he had the movement and activity level of someone who was probably fifty. Jack could only hope to age as well as him and his father before him, who had just died five years ago at the venerable age of ninety-nine years.

"Good evening, Father. It's good to see you."

Father came around the desk and embraced Jack tightly for a moment. Jack felt like a boy of five again with the smell of ink and his father's sandalwood soap crowding his senses. "Good to see you too."

They parted, and Father gestured for him to sit in one of the wingback chairs angled before the hearth, where a low fire burned on this cool April evening. As Jack took his usual chair, Father went to the sideboard and poured two glasses of his favorite whisky, which he procured every fall when he traveled to Scotland to hunt.

A moment later, his father handed him a glass and sat opposite him. They both raised their whisky in silent toast before taking simultaneous sips. How many times had they done precisely this? Far too many to count, and Jack hoped there would still be far more than he could imagine.

"You've been busy since Parliament opened," Father said over the rim of his glass.

Jack winced inwardly. "Yes, sorry I haven't been to visit."

His father waved his hand. "I don't care about that. With everything going on, I can well imagine how overwhelming it's all been. The riots last fall, the attack on the Prince Regent, the march from Manchester... That's a great deal to manage in the best of times."

"As you know from personal experience, this is not the best of times."

His father had been an MP for several years until Jack had taken over in the last election. Before him, Jack's grandfather, for whom Jack had been named, had been MP. Barretts had occupied this seat for decades. That was a detail the rotten-borough MPs liked to point out to Jack when he discussed the overwhelming corruption in so many constituencies.

"Yes, and it seems the Tories are reacting just as they always do, with fear and a need to maintain their grip however they can." Father shook his head before sipping his whisky once more.

"It may be even worse than that," Jack said darkly. He'd thought about this mystery MP he and Lady Viola were hunting, and was nearly convinced it was a Tory trying to foment fear and distrust toward the radicals and workers and anyone else in opposition to them. "Apparently, an MP advised a group of radicals—or maybe it was one radical, I don't know the details—to attack the Prince Regent. He told them where the prince would be and when to attack him. I suspect it's a Tory trying to instigate the radicals in order to stoke fear so Parliament would implement a secret committee or suspend habeas corpus, which it did." Jack scowled.

James Barrett was a difficult man to upset—unflappable was the word that came to mind when describing him. But now he seemed to freeze, his eyes locking on Jack. "An MP was behind the attack?" Jack nodded, and his father continued. "You know it was a Tory?"

"Not for certain—I don't know the person's identity at all. I am trying to find out, though."

Father's brow creased and his mouth settled into a deep frown. "You must be careful, Jack. If it is a Tory, they have power right now, and you'll only make trouble for yourself if you dig into things. But what if it isn't a Tory? Doesn't it make as much sense that a sympathetic MP could be trying to aid the radicals?"

"What would attacking the Prince actually gain them? No, it has to be a Tory."

Father chuckled softly. "You're assuming this MP is as cunning as you are. Many of them are not."

Wasn't that the truth? Sir Humphrey came to mind. His idiocy was almost canceled out by his good friend Caldwell's clever deviousness. Almost.

"How did you hear of this?" Father asked.

"It's gossip for now." At his father's dark look, Jack waved him off. "Don't give me that expression. I am hunting down the truth. Hodges heard it, and he's trustworthy."

"Yes, but he's also starting to go deaf, though he covers for it very well," Father said wryly. "While I understand your desire to find the truth of the matter, aren't your energies better spent elsewhere? You've built a good career for yourself over the past four and a half years, and as far as I can tell, you could spend the next several decades representing Middlesex." A small smile crept across his father's lips. "Unless you're elevated to the peerage, of course. Then you'll still represent us, just in a different place."

Jack nearly groaned. That was Father's goal for him. "I am quite content in the House of Commons, and will be honored to represent Middlesex for as long as they will have me."

"Perhaps you should consider taking a wife."

The whisky Jack had just sipped nearly shot straight out of his mouth. Instead, Jack choked on it, the fiery liquid burning his throat. When he was finished sputtering, he stared at his father. "I beg your pardon?"

His father's eyes narrowed shrewdly. "You heard me."

"I'm afraid I did. Why on earth would you suggest that? You just said I'm doing well, and you know I'm only thirty."

"Yes, you're thirty, and I know you've stated you

won't wed until you're thirty-five because that's what your grandfather and I did. We are not role models in this sense."

Jack couldn't have disagreed more. "You and Grandfather are the best role models—in every sense."

Father sipped his whisky and stared into the fireplace for a moment. When he looked back to Jack, his smile was sad, his gaze weary. "I regret waiting so long. I actually met your mother just after I became a barrister. I was twenty-two years old and full of vigor —and arrogance. It was clear that we suited. I loved her, but not as much as my ambition. The next part you know: she married someone else and after he died, we wed." Father inched forward in his chair, his eyes intense. "I lost over a decade with her. When I think of that time and the other children we could have had…"

The fact that his father had rejected his mother sat in Jack's gut like a stone. "I haven't met anyone like Mother," he said quietly. "What I mean to say is that I haven't met anyone I would like to wed."

An image of Lady Viola sprang forth in his mind. Why should he think of her? Because he enjoyed her company and found her attractive. Regardless, he absolutely hadn't considered marrying her and had no intention to.

"You also aren't open to the idea." Father sat back in his chair, cradling his whisky glass between his hands. "I'm merely suggesting you consider the possibility. Don't live your life by an arbitrary timeline, and don't let your career override everything." His mouth tilted sardonically. "It won't keep you warm at night."

The discomfort swirling in Jack's belly grew until he knew he had to change the topic. He was saved from having to do so by the arrival of Michaelson announcing dinner.

They finished their whisky and stood from their chairs. Father clapped Jack on the shoulder. "I'm proud of you, son. You know I'll support you, no matter what. Just promise me you'll be careful with this attack business. I hope you'll take my advice and steer far clear of it. Trouble has a way of finding us. There's no need to go looking for it."

Father set his glass on the sideboard and quit the library. Jack followed suit, his mind churning with what he'd just learned and his father's counsel. Perhaps he should let this investigation go.

But that would mean leaving Lady Viola to continue on her own, and that wasn't safe either. If it was dangerous for Jack, it was especially so for her. If this really was a Tory plot, they'd have no compunction about harming someone like her—or Tavistock, in this case—not after they'd already attacked the bloody Prince Regent.

It was time to sit down with her and have a frank discussion about what she intended to do if they learned the truth—and whether they should walk away now, while they still could.

∾

*T*he traffic in the park was terrible. Viola suspected Grandmama's barouche had moved approximately ten feet in the past quarter hour. The day was overcast but fair, and so everyone was out, or so it seemed. Of course, they'd move more quickly if they weren't constantly waylaid by Grandmama's friends and acquaintances. Everyone— well, not *everyone*—sought the dowager's favor.

At last, Grandmama waved off whomever she'd been chatting with, and the barouche moved forward. Viola must have made some sound of relief, as Grandmama gave her a pointed stare.

"Are you bored?" she asked.

"Yes, actually." Viola saw no point in prevaricating. "Perhaps I'll get out for a walk. I see Felicity."

"Before you go, I want to speak with you about the ball tonight."

Viola kept herself from visibly cringing. Tonight was the Goodrick ball, and Viola wished she could beg off. Or come down with malaria. Perhaps she could sprain her foot descending from the barouche.

Except any social event was an opportunity to hear something—anything—about the MP who'd instigated the attack on the Prince Regent.

"I'm quite looking forward to it." *That* Viola would lie about.

"No, you aren't, but I do appreciate the effort you are putting in since I mentioned you should return to the Marriage Mart. Tonight shall be your triumphant reentry."

Good God, what did that mean? Was Grandmama going to hang a sign about her neck? Of course not. She'd never do something so vulgar. "You want me to have a dance card?" She cringed, waiting for the dowager's response.

"Yes. There are plenty of excellent matches to be made. Take Lord Orford, for instance. He is widowed, and he has a young child."

"Therefore, he must be in need of a wife," Viola muttered.

"*Yes.*" Grandmama's eyes narrowed with annoyance. "If you behave as though you don't wish to wed or that you think the entire endeavor is beneath you, there will be no success in your future. Do you wish to remain unmarried?"

Desperately. "I am quite content in my current state." She smiled serenely for added effect.

Grandmama blew out a breath in frustration. "I will not be here forever. Who will take care of you after I am gone? Val is married now, and you can't expect to impose on him. Well, you could, I suppose, but I daresay you wouldn't want to."

Heavens *no*. "I suspect I can take care of myself, just as you have done since Grandpapa died."

"It would be different, my dear. I had children and grandchildren. You will have no one." She waved her hand. "Go and walk, then. Tonight you will dance, and you will entertain the *possibility* of marriage."

"Yes, Grandmama." Viola nodded, then reached for the handle of the barouche. The footman on the back jumped down and helped Viola descend.

As she made her way toward Felicity along the pedestrian path, she felt a mixture of irritation and sadness. Grandmama was right—Viola wouldn't have anyone after she was gone. Oh, she could be an aunt to Val's children, assuming he had any, but it wasn't the same as having her own husband and children. Plus, Grandmama was right in that she would never want to intrude.

"Viola!" Felicity waved as Viola approached. Grinning, she greeted her friend warmly, then immediately sobered. "What's wrong?"

"Grandmama says I must have a dance card this evening."

Felicity made a face that was part outrage and part disdain. "Well, that's upsetting."

"She says I must consider the *possibility* of marriage."

"That isn't so bad," Felicity said brightly. She took Viola's hand. "Let us consider it together." She pursed her lips and furrowed her brow as if she were thinking intently. "Are you considering it?"

Viola fought not to laugh. "I'm doing my best."

Felicity held her breath and seemed to concentrate even harder. When her cheeks turned red, Viola couldn't stand it another moment and burst out laughing. Felicity exhaled, her lungs emptying in a whoosh. "I've given it my very best, and I'm afraid marriage just may not be in the offing for you." She gave Viola a pitying look. "My gravest apologies."

Viola dissolved into more laughter, and Felicity finally cracked, joining her.

"You two ladies look as if you're having a grand time."

Viola and Felicity swung their heads in unison, their laughter halting like a spigot stopping the flow of ale from a cask. Lord Orford regarded them with his pale gray eyes, his thin lips spread in a smile as he presented his leg.

They curtsied in return and exchanged glances. Felicity thrust her arm through Viola's, perhaps to deter him from asking them to promenade. "Good afternoon, Lord Orford."

"Good afternoon, Lady Viola, Lady Felicity. Perhaps you'd care to promenade with me." With certain gentlemen, deterrence rarely worked, unfortunately.

"Both of us?" Viola asked. She didn't want to abandon Felicity to him nor did she want to walk with him alone.

"Why not?" He offered his arms.

Felicity and Viola traded another look and answered with imperceptible shrugs. They each took one of his well-muscled arms—Lord Orford was known to enjoy pugilism—and started along the path.

"Please tell me you will both be at the Goodrick ball this evening so that I may sign both of your dance cards."

"Er, yes," Felicity said haltingly. She leaned forward and cast Viola a look of apology.

Viola rolled her eyes and gave her head a tiny

shake, trying to communicate that it didn't matter. She may as well dance with Lord Orford as anyone.

But she'd rather dance with Jack Barrett.

Good Lord, where had that thought come from? From the dark corner of her mind, apparently, and it could go right back there.

Searching for something to occupy her errant brain, Viola realized Lord Orford was a member of the House of Commons. He was the Viscount Orford, but it was a courtesy title. He sat in the Commons, while his father, the Earl of Debenham, sat in the House of Lords. Perhaps Orford could be helpful...

"What news from the House of Commons, my lord?" she asked prettily.

He looked down at her, a slightly perplexed glint in his eyes. "You can't possibly be interested in such things."

Viola resisted the urge to trip him. She did, however, grind her teeth together behind her tightened lips. Felicity shot her a look that reflected Viola's irritation.

"Why not?" Viola asked. "I like to be informed. All this business with the march in Manchester and the riots last fall. Every citizen should be aware of what is happening. I should dearly love to know what happened with the attack on the Prince Regent. I can't help thinking there is more to that incident. Why don't we know who was behind it?"

Viola watched his face for the slightest inclination that he might know something. Had his eye twitched? Yes, she thought maybe it had.

He waved his hand before his face, and she saw the insect he batted away. Perhaps that was the reason for the spasm. Or not.

He frowned deeply. "That was a dastardly incursion. Whoever was responsible should be hanged."

"Shouldn't they be arrested first? Tried, perhaps?" Felicity said.

"Yes, of course. I said the responsible party should be punished, and the word *responsible* presumes they are guilty."

Viola couldn't help pushing him to see where he stood. "The suspension of habeas corpus is dangerous."

"I don't disagree. However, these are dangerous times, and we must keep everyone safe. I'd much rather suspected radicals are removed from the streets than left to organize another attack such as the one against the Prince Regent."

"What if the radicals didn't organize it?" Viola asked. "I mean, we don't really know, do we?"

Felicity peered at her around the viscount, her gaze sparking with curiosity.

Lord Orford shot Viola a look of amusement. Amusement? He found her funny? "What have you heard, Lady Viola?"

The question took her by surprise. It seemed so... pointed. As if he knew she was referring to gossip she'd heard. Which, of course, she was. And now she presumed he'd heard it too. "I don't know, what have *you* heard?" she asked coyly.

He narrowed his eyes for the barest moment—so briefly, she wondered if she'd imagined it, just as she'd wondered if she'd imagined the twitch. Then his attention snapped to somewhere down the path. "I'm afraid you'll have to excuse me, ladies. I look forward to seeing you later." He bowed to each of them as they withdrew their arms.

"What was that about?" Felicity asked while they watched him depart.

"Oh, nothing," Viola said, turning to return the way they'd come.

Felicity pivoted with her. "The attack on Prinny

isn't 'nothing.' Why were you asking Orford about it?"

Viola shrugged. "I just thought he might be in a position to know something. Wouldn't you like to know what happened?"

"We *do* know what happened. Some idiotic people shot at—or threw rocks, depending on whom you ask—the Prince Regent. I would like those people to be in prison so they can't try again, but that doesn't seem likely at this point."

Viola didn't agree with that observation, but then she knew more than Felicity on the matter. Perhaps she could confide in her...

"There's my brother and Diana," Felicity said. "I'll see you tonight." She clasped Viola's hand and gave it a squeeze. "I am not above helping you come down with a ghastly illness or injury if you need it." She winked at Viola and walked toward the Duke and Duchess of Colehaven.

Pensive after the conversation with Lord Orford, Viola looked down at the path as she took a few steps.

"Careful, there." Strong hands clasped her elbows for a slight moment.

Awareness flashed through her. She knew that voice, that touch. Snapping her head up, she looked into the captivating walnut-colored eyes of Jack Barrett.

His hands were gone before she could begin to appreciate their warmth and security. Appreciate? She was going daft in the head.

"Good afternoon, Mr. Barrett," she said.

"Good afternoon, Lady Viola. May I walk with you?" he asked.

"Yes, I'm just on my way back to my grandmother in her barouche."

He offered his arm, and she grasped his sleeve. "I

think we should visit the coffeehouse again," she said without preamble.

"How are you today?" Mr. Barrett asked in a mockingly overinterested tone. "The weather is quite fine. Did you walk or ride to the park?"

She glanced over at him with a guilty smile. "Sorry. How are you today?"

"Very well, thank you. As to visiting the coffeehouse, I actually think we should consider abandoning our inquiries."

Viola stopped and stared at him. "Why?"

"It's a dangerous endeavor. We're seeking a man who had no compunction about harming the Prince Regent. I doubt they would hesitate to commit violence against us."

While that was true, Viola refused to be afraid. She was also disappointed in his change of heart. "The truth should be known. I thought you agreed with that."

"I did. I do. But we are perhaps not the best people to investigate this situation."

"If not us—no, not us, *me*—if not me, who?" She scowled at him and withdrew her arm from his. "Never mind. I don't need your help. And before you threaten to tell my brother, I'll tell him myself if I must."

He expelled a breath. "You don't need to do that. But will you please think about what I said? I understand how important it is to you to uncover this information and make it known, but surely there are other articles you can write."

Nothing as consequential as this. She understood his concern, but this was too important. "I'll think about what you said." While she planned her next move—alone.

Mr. Barrett's eyes narrowed skeptically. "Do I

need to worry you'll show up at Brooks's again tonight? I plan to be there, just so you know."

Viola rolled her eyes, then started walking along the path toward her grandmother's barouche. She'd looped around and was now on her way back. "You do not need to concern yourself. I will be at a ball with my grandmother tonight." Dancing. The thought of it turned her stomach. And to think, she'd considered what it might be like to dance with Mr. Barrett! Right now, she'd like to tread all over his arrogant toes.

"What ball?" Mr. Barrett asked.

"Lady Goodrick's," Viola answered absentmindedly as she caught sight of her grandmother waving for her to come back to the barouche. "I'm afraid I must go. Thank you for this—*informative* —promenade."

"Please don't be angry with me. I only care about your well-being."

She nodded, understanding but still feeling betrayed by his second thoughts. Turning, she returned to the barouche, where her grandmother was looking toward Mr. Barrett.

"Whom were you walking with?" Grandmama asked.

"Mr. Jack Barrett."

"The barrister? No, he used to be a barrister and now he's an MP. Barretts always hold that Middlesex seat."

Viola blinked at her. "Grandmama, do you know everyone? Don't answer that. I know you do."

"I know his father. He was also a barrister and an MP and quite a brilliant legal mind. Your grandfather worked with him in Parliament on a few matters." Grandmama fixed her with an expectant stare. "How do you know Mr. Barrett?"

"I believe Val introduced him to me."

"Are you really going to make me squeeze every bit of information from you as if I were trying to take the juice from a lemon? Why were you walking with him?"

"Because he was there?" Viola knew what her grandmother was after. "He is not a suitor."

"Good. You can do far better."

That was another reason she resisted marriage. When she'd accepted Edmund's proposal, she'd done so in part because of who he was—the son of a prominent duke. In hindsight, a man of his rank was never going to be a good match for her.

"What if I don't want to?" she asked quietly, glancing down at her lap before looking back at her grandmother.

Grandmama's eyes widened. "Do you have a... tendre for the MP?"

"No!" She answered quickly and vehemently. "I only meant, what if I consider marriage, as you suggested," *demanded* was a more accurate description, "and actually find someone I might like to wed, and he doesn't have a title?"

"I suppose that depends on who he is. If he's a blacksmith, absolutely not. Your brother might keep company with such people at his *tavern*, but you shall not." If only Grandmama knew, Viola thought as the dowager continued, "An MP *might* be acceptable."

Well, that was good to know. As well as pointless. Because no matter how badly her grandmother wanted her to marry, Viola wanted even more fiercely to remain unwed.

ere unmarried women allowed to wear that color? Jack couldn't help but stare —covertly—at Lady Viola garbed in a vivid puce gown that bordered on red. It was an astonishing color that drew the eye, and the woman wearing it kept the onlooker's attention. With her honey-blonde hair dressed in an elegant coiffure and her form perfectly draped in the gown that accentuated the slender angle of her shoulder and the swell of her bosom, she was a vision of feminine loveliness, a far cry from Tavistock.

"Evening, Barrett. Don't usually see you at a ball."

Jack turned to see his friend Adam Chamberlain, a former MP from Lancashire who now sat in the House of Lords as the Viscount Whitworth. "Not usually, no. How are you, Whitworth?"

"Excellent, thank you. On the hunt for a viscountess this Season."

"Glad I don't have to worry about begetting an heir," Jack said with a grin.

"Oh, but there's fun in trying, isn't there?" Whitworth chortled. He squinted toward the other side of the ballroom. "Who is that beauty in the puce gown?"

"Lady Viola Fairfax, I believe."

Whitworth winced, his mouth pulling into a grimace. "Never mind that, then."

Jack turned to stare at the man, outrage rising in his chest. "What do you mean?"

"She's not someone I'd consider. I'd have to expect she'd abandon me on our wedding day just as she did poor Ledbury."

She'd been betrothed to the Earl of Ledbury? How had Jack not known this?

Because you don't give a fig about Society and their nonsense. The better question is why would you have known?

"I'm sure she had good reason not to marry him," Jack said, despite not having the slightest idea what that could be. He didn't know Ledbury well, but he seemed a pleasant enough fellow, dedicated to his work in the House of Commons and charming to a fault.

Whitworth's brows arched. "You know her?"

Damn. "Not well. I simply presume she had good reason. What lady would voluntarily put herself in the position of crying off unless she saw no other alternative?"

"I suppose." Whitworth's shrug and skeptical gaze said the opposite, but thankfully, another gentleman approached, and the conversation died a well-deserved death.

Jack excused himself a moment later and gradually made his way to the corner where Lady Viola stood speaking with another woman. He bowed to them when he arrived. "Good evening."

Lady Viola eyed him with surprise. "Good evening, Mr. Barrett. Allow me to present my sister-in-law, Her Grace, the Duchess of Eastleigh."

"I'm pleased to make your acquaintance, Your Grace." Jack inclined his head toward the tall beauty.

"As I am, Mr. Barrett. We met very briefly about a

decade ago at Oxford. My father was warden of
Merton College. "

Jack's jaw dropped for a moment. "I'm very
pleased to make your acquaintance. Your father was
brilliant."

Light swaths of pink washed her cheeks. "Thank
you. I think so too."

Now that he'd formally made her acquaintance,
Jack recalled Eastleigh mentioning that they'd met at
Oxford. He really needed not only to pay more attention to social information—he needed to remember
it. Particularly when it concerned his friends.

Jack turned his attention to Lady Viola. "I came to
ask if you'd like to dance."

"No." She looked as though he'd asked her to clean
his boots after he'd trudged through a dung-laden
field. She hastened to add, "Thank you."

Her Grace smiled even as she sent Viola a somewhat stern look. "What Viola means to say is that she
doesn't particularly care to dance right *now*."

Lady Viola nearly scowled—Jack watched her
mouth tighten, and then she seemed to force herself
to slowly relax, her lips loosening but not quite ele-
vating into a smile. He tried not to laugh. "Yes, that's
what I meant to say. I should like to promenade,
however."

"Excellent." He offered her his arm and nodded
toward the duchess. "Please excuse us."

When they were several steps away, he felt Lady
Viola relax. Not completely, but enough that he realized just how tense she'd been. "Do you not like
dancing?"

"Not particularly. I've successfully avoided it almost entirely the past several years." Her muscles
tensed again. "My grandmother has decided it's time
I get back to it."

Jack surveyed the ballroom in search of the

Dowager Duchess of Eastleigh. Petite, with hair the color of snow and a stare that could make a man's bollocks shrink to the size of peas, she was an intimidating force. He'd met her only once and had decided he hadn't needed to repeat the experience.

Only now, he was promenading with the woman's granddaughter. Just what the hell was he doing with the sister of a duke?

"I'm surprised to see you here," Lady Viola said, glancing at him from the corner of her eye. "I thought you said you were going to be at Brooks's."

"So I did. However, I found I was unable to avoid coming here first once I knew you would be in attendance."

"Please say you aren't flirting with me."

"Blo—*no*." He caught himself before swearing. "Don't take that personally. I don't flirt. With anyone." Except he wondered if maybe he was.

"Me neither. What would be the point?"

He nearly laughed again, then shot her an admiring look. "Indeed. If your grandmother wants you to dance, is she hoping you'll do something else?"

"Marry, you mean?" Lady Viola's features tightened, her brow furrowing and the flesh around her mouth pulling. In profile, she looked decidedly perturbed.

"Can't a woman dance without being expected to marry?" he asked.

She stopped and turned her head to stare at him. After a moment, she said, her voice barely audible, as if she were astounded by his query. "*Yes*. That exactly." She started walking again.

He guided her along the perimeter of the ballroom, steering clear of other ball goers. "Is that why you hate to dance?"

"Probably. There are always expectations. If not marriage, then some anticipation or assumption is made depending on whom I danced with and how many sets I danced." She rolled her eyes. "It's exhausting."

"I think you find it more than exhausting," he said with a hint of a smile.

"Mr. Barrett, I daresay you are coming to know me far too well." She peered over at him in mock alarm.

"I disagree. There is much I don't know about you. For instance, I just tonight learned you were betrothed before." A flush started up her neck, and he immediately regretted indulging his curiosity. "Never mind that I mentioned that. Please."

She lifted the shoulder of the arm entwined with his. "It's all right. That happened so long ago. Scarcely anyone mentions it anymore. I'm surprised you just now heard of it."

He heard a question there—why had someone brought it up now? "I was admiring you across the ballroom." He didn't mention that he wasn't alone in doing so or that the other man had been the one to point out her "failings."

"You were?" The question came out higher than she usually spoke, and much higher than the voice she used as Tavistock.

"It's difficult not to—your gown is striking." As was her hair, the graceful column of her neck, the slope of her breast. He worked to banish such thoughts.

"Thank you." She paused near the doors leading to the terrace. "May we step outside for a moment? I'm feeling a trifle overheated."

"Of course." He led her onto the balcony that overlooked the walled garden. They strolled to the railing, and she withdrew her arm from his. He found he missed her touch. That had never happened before.

She was quiet a moment as she stared out over the garden. Then she turned to face him. He hadn't even pivoted toward the railing—his body had remained aligned completely toward hers, like a sprout seeking the sun.

"I can tell you're dying to know what happened with my betrothal."

He found amusement in her statement. "How can you tell?"

Her gaze settled briefly between his eyes. "The top of your nose scrunches up into little lines when you are particularly interested in something. I've noticed it several times in the course of our association."

"Does it?" Reflexively, he touched the bridge of his nose. "It seems you are coming to know me very well too," he murmured, thinking that must certainly be an extraordinary occurrence. Had a woman ever known him well enough to recognize a tiny facial expression that he wasn't even aware of?

She didn't respond, so he said, "Yes, I would like to know what happened, but you needn't tell me. Clearly, Ledbury is an ass."

A glorious laugh leapt from her lips, and she clapped a gloved hand over her mouth. Her eyes danced in the moonlight. He was utterly captivated.

"He wasn't really an *ass*," she said after lowering her hand. "He just wasn't for me. As I prepared for the ceremony at the church, I realized I'd never be able to write anything for publication—not for a newspaper, not a pamphlet, not a book. He said a countess couldn't do such a thing. At least not *his* countess. I would cease to exist as Viola Fairfax the moment I became the Countess of Ledbury. I just couldn't do it." She sounded a trifle sad, but not regretful. "Perhaps he was a *bit* of an ass."

More than a bit in Jack's estimation. "When I get

around to marrying, I would hope my wife would retain her sense of self. She might be Mrs. Barrett, but the woman she was when we wed would forever be the woman I fell in love with." He coughed, feeling slightly uncomfortable all of a sudden. "If I'm lucky enough to fall in love as my parents did."

Lady Viola's gaze had softened while he spoke. "My parents were fond of each other, but I don't think their emotions ran deeper than that. My brother is desperately in love with his wife. It's nice to see." She shook her head. "Not *nice*. Powerful. Moving. Intoxicating."

Jack felt a little drunk at the moment. The urge to kiss her swept over him, at once shocking and thrilling.

The air between them seemed to thin. Accordingly, their breathing grew rapid, and it was all he could hear. She was all he could see...

"We should go back inside." She broke the spell with those five sensible words.

Taking a deep breath to calm his racing heart, Jack offered her his arm once more. "Ledbury must have been very sorry when you decided not to marry him."

"I think he was relieved. His father and my grandmother had orchestrated the match, and while I liked him and he liked me, there was no danger of a broken heart on either side."

Something in Jack's chest pinched. He ignored the sensation. "I've changed my mind about our investigation. I think we should go to Brooks's on Monday evening."

She paused at the threshold before they stepped back into the ballroom. "You do?"

"I still think it's dangerous, but it's too important to ignore." He'd been pondering it since seeing her that afternoon, but their conversation on the terrace had persuaded him. She wanted this. She deserved this. And he would help her see it through.

She squeezed his arm. "Thank you. Truly."

Another couple came to the doorway, and Jack swiftly guided Lady Viola inside. "You'll come as my guest, and we'll do what you'd planned with Pennington—we'll just keep our ears open and find out what we can."

"What if we act as though we already know who the MP is?" she suggested softly, her tone rife with anticipation. "We can mention the gossip and then be coy about identifying the MP. Just like everyone else has done," she added wryly.

"You think Pennington lied, that he knew more than he revealed?"

She shrugged. "I think it's possible. I also think it's possible Hodges knew more. We should probably visit him again too."

"Probably. I'm just a trifle nervous about Tavistock being seen as pursuing this story."

"I thought about that, actually. Today I managed to turn the conversation to this topic with a gentleman in the park."

Now Jack stopped as apprehension twisted through him. "Whom did you talk to?" He wasn't sure what he was afraid to hear—there wasn't anyone he feared. Except everyone when it came to her safety. Good Lord, what was going on with him?

"Lord Orford. He didn't seem to know anything."

Jack snorted in disgust. "Orford wouldn't. He's from a rotten borough amidst other rotten boroughs paid for by his father. He only pays attention to matters his father cares about." He looked at her seriously. "You must promise not to do that again. It's bad enough that Tavistock is out there making inquiries. Lady Viola Fairfax shouldn't be doing that too."

She nodded. "I will be careful." Her gaze narrowed slightly. "My grandmother is staring at me. She's going to ask why I promenaded with you instead of danced."

"Tell her I have an injury that prevents such activity."

She grinned, and the desire to kiss her crashed into him anew. "Brilliant."

He needed to get the hell away from her before he did something incredibly foolish such as tell her what he wanted. "I'll meet you Monday at the entrance to your mews. Nine o'clock."

She nodded. "I'll look forward to it." Her cerulean eyes glowed beneath the hundreds of candles overhead.

Jack was looking forward to it too—probably more than anything he had in a long, long time.

CHAPTER 8

On Monday evening, Viola stepped down from the hack after Mr. Barrett and straightened her coat. He stared at her puce waistcoat. "I should have made you change."

She smoothed a hand over her front. "Why? I love how this turned out. Yes, I know it's the same color as my gown on Saturday, but will anyone really notice?" She didn't wait for him to answer. "Well, if they do, it just means Mr. Tavistock shops at the same linen draper as Lady Viola Fairfax."

Jack rolled his eyes. "Arguing with you is often an exercise in complete futility."

"You're learning! Excellent." She flashed him a sardonic smile and started toward the entrance to Brooks's.

The entry hall was grand, with white marble floors and the signature staircase climbing the right wall. She wondered what was up there while acknowledging she'd likely never find out. The fact that she was in here at all was astonishing.

As with her last visit, the sense of adventure filled her with excitement and anticipation. This was even better than that time because she wasn't alone. Mr. Barrett made her feel...safer.

They spent the next several minutes greeting various gentlemen as they made their way to the subscription room. Mr. Barrett leaned over and whispered, "I see Pennington over in the corner. Let's make our way in that direction."

She nodded in response, and they started across the room. Another gentleman stopped Mr. Barrett and began speaking with him. Viola didn't particularly want to meet someone else, especially since the man seemed rather intent on Mr. Barrett and only Mr. Barrett. Pivoting, she made to continue toward Pennington and nearly ran into someone else.

"I beg your pardon." The Earl of Ledbury—Edmund—looked down at her, his once-familiar dark gaze tinged with apology. "I wasn't looking where I was going, I'm afraid."

He studied her, and her pulse raced to a frenetic pace. Was he going to recognize her? She was confident the whiskers sufficiently disguised her femininity. Although, Mr. Barrett hadn't been fooled. She reasoned she was safe so long as she didn't present her backside.

"It's quite all right," she said, lowering her voice even more than usual in her apprehension.

"Have we met before?" Edmund continued to peruse her, his eyes taking on a hint of confusion.

"Not sure we have. I'm Tavistock."

"Ledbury," he said. "You seem familiar, so I'm certain we must have met. I'm just trying to think of where…"

Viola's insides were screaming with alarm. She had to get away from him!

"Good evening, Ledbury." The smooth, sanguine tone of Mr. Barrett's voice calmed her—at least partially. "I see you've met Tavistock."

"Yes, though I'm sure we've met before this." Edmund shook his head. "It doesn't matter. Pleased to meet you, Tavistock."

Viola inclined her head.

"Brandy, then?" Mr. Barrett asked her.

"Definitely."

They excused themselves from Ledbury and continued on their way. Partway to Pennington, Mr. Barrett slowed. "I'm sorry I left you alone."

"You didn't. I walked off." She shook her head in self-admonition. "I won't be doing that again while we're here."

"He seemed to think he knew you. Have you ever met him as Tavistock?"

She shook her head. "He doesn't come to the Wicked Duke, of course. Since Val owns it. *That* would be awkward."

"Do you think he recognized *you?*"

"No, but I admit I was alarmed for a moment there. All this time, I thought my disguise was so thorough. But you saw through it." Heat rushed over her, and she feared her cheeks were scarlet. "Shall we go see Pennington?" Her voice had risen slightly out of her Tavistock range. She mentally chided herself for such foolishness.

"Good plan. Yes, let's see Pennington."

They arrived at Pennington's table without further incident. He sat with two other gentlemen.

"Tavistock, Barrett!" Pennington greeted them with a grin. "Sit with us. You must know Naylor and Yates."

"Of course," Mr. Barrett said, taking a seat.

For a moment, Viola waited for him to hold her chair before realizing she was supposed to be a bloody man. She sat down with alacrity and hoped there would be brandy forthwith. She needed just a sip or two to calm her nerves. Because of Ledbury.

Yes, of course because of Ledbury.

Or the fact that you're dressed as a man at Brooks's.
Nothing to do with Jack Barrett. Nothing at all.

The brandy did indeed arrive shortly, and Viola took two small sips. Then she did her best to join in the conversation about horseflesh. After a while, Naylor and Yates took their leave. Viola exchanged a look with Mr. Barrett, who gave her a very slight nod. That meant she should do what they'd discussed.

"Pennington," she started, "I visited with Hodges the other day at the coffeehouse. He told me all about that...*incident.*" She arched her brows before picking up her glass and pretending to take another drink. Acting as though she were drinking as much as her companions was an important part of her masquerade.

Pennington stuck his lips out and narrowed his eyes before realization struck. "Oh! The *incident.* He told you *all* about it?"

She nodded. "He did. So fascinating."

"Did he tell you as well?" Pennington asked Mr. Barrett.

"No, but Tavistock shared the details. It's bloody shocking to think that happened."

The color in Pennington's face lightened. He shifted in his chair. "I hope you aren't sharing this with anyone else. I shouldn't have said anything to you at the Wicked Duke. I hope you haven't told anyone that I did."

The man sounded...afraid. Viola exchanged another glance with Mr. Barrett, who seemed to share her concern.

"No, we haven't told anyone," Viola said evenly. "However, you know I'm a reporter."

Pennington flinched. "Yes. Well, whatever you write, I do hope you'll keep my name out of it."

"Of course," Mr. Barrett said. "This is a...sensitive

issue. Your identity isn't important, just that of the MP."

"Do you know who he is?" Pennington looked between them, his gaze a mixture of curiosity and dread.

"Don't you?" Mr. Barrett countered before Viola could form a response.

Pennington shook his head. "Thankfully, no. I think it's only a matter of time before he's arrested."

Mr. Barrett leaned forward. "Why do you think that?"

Draining his brandy glass, Pennington set it back on the table and abruptly stood. "If you'll excuse me, I've somewhere I need to be."

And then he was gone, stalking away as if the club was on fire.

"What do you suppose has him so frightened?" she whispered, turning toward Mr. Barrett.

"I'm not sure, but it's concerning to say the least. I wish he'd answered that last question. Does he know something that leads him to believe this MP will be arrested? Or was he simply prognosticating?" Mr. Barrett tapped his finger on the table. "Given his reaction, I'm not sure I want to continue this tack tonight. I think we should go."

Disappointment curled through Viola, and yet she didn't disagree. The encounter with Edmund had put her on edge, and Pennington's odd behavior had only intensified her feeling of unease.

They stood and left the subscription room quickly, not stopping to chat with anyone. Outside, Mr. Barrett hailed a hack and gave the driver the direction of her mews.

"I'll drop you at home before I continue on to the Wicked Duke," Mr. Barrett said, sitting beside her since this vehicle had only the one seat.

"Do you ever go home?" she asked.

"Yes."

"Where is that?"

"King Street, on the edge of St. James's Square."

Outside Mayfair. Still a fashionable location, but she was suddenly aware of the divide between them —her a duke's sister and him a barrister and MP. "Did you like being a barrister, or do you prefer being an MP?" she asked.

He seemed startled by her question, and she supposed it had seemed to come out of nowhere. "I was just thinking how different we are," she said. "And yet not," she added softly.

He turned toward her on the seat. "I prefer being an MP. I like making a difference for people. My grandfather and my father were both MPs before me. I'm honored to continue their legacy."

She could see that. He was a man of dignity and pride, but not arrogantly so. At least not excessively arrogant. A dash of arrogance was rather attractive, she decided. Or maybe it was just that Jack Barrett was attractive.

Lines around his mouth creased. "We should probably stop doing this. That business with Ledbury was damn close. It's only a matter of time before someone discovers you're a woman."

"You mean someone besides you."

His eyes were darker than the night around them, but full of intense energy. "Yes. And then you'll be in real trouble."

"What kind of trouble?" The question tumbled from her, sounding breathless and expectant.

"Scandal. Ruination. Desire."

Her heart picked up speed. "Desire?"

"You are a very attractive woman, even with that bloody disguise. If anyone paid close attention to you, they'd find themselves beguiled."

"Are you?" she asked softly.

He leaned close, his face so near that she could see the faint stubble of his beard beginning to shadow his jaw. "Irrevocably."

His head dipped down, and she quickly reached up with both hands and pulled the sideburns from her face. She winced slightly at the brief sting—she normally didn't tear them off like that—as she stuffed the disguise in her coat pocket.

His brow arched. "Better." Then his hands came up and cupped her face, his thumbs tracing along her sensitive skin where the whiskers had been.

Frowning, he withdrew his hands, and she feared he'd changed his mind. Disappointment curdled in her belly, pushing away the desire. Then she realized he was removing his gloves. His hands returned, bare this time, and the touch of his thumb against her cheeks and jaw brought the desire rushing back.

"Better," she murmured, echoing him, allowing her eyelids to droop as his mouth pressed against hers.

She'd kissed Edmund, of course, quite passionately, or so she'd thought. It had been rather pleasant, but this was not how she'd describe the feel of Mr. Barrett's—Jack's, because how could she think of Edmund as Edmund and not Jack as Jack?—lips on hers.

He kissed her softly, his mouth lingering with a gentle caress. Then he angled his head the other way and kissed her again. Still, he repositioned himself and teased her once more, a featherlight kiss that did everything to stoke her desire and nothing to satisfy it.

She clasped the back of his neck and held him still as she kissed him more firmly than he'd dared. Sealing her mouth against his, she parted her lips. His tongue swept inside, and it was as if an invisible barrier fell away.

He cupped the back of her head, knocking her hat

off with one hand. Rising over her, he forced her back gently as he drove into her mouth. His other hand drifted down her neck and over her chest, then found its way inside her coat, where it flattened against her waistcoat. Yes, this was what she'd wanted, what she'd *missed*. No, she hadn't missed it because she'd never had it. She simply couldn't compare him to Edmund. She was drawn to this man in this coach as she'd been to no other.

The kiss ended only to begin again with even greater fervor. She curled her hands into the hair at his nape and dislodged his hat. She'd no notion where it went, only that his head was bare and she could rake her fingers through his thick hair.

His hand pushed up against her breast, which was bound beneath a length of muslin. She'd never regretted her costuming choices in the past, but tonight, she was desperate to be a woman.

Eager for more of his touch, she strained against him, bringing one hand down to his shoulder and gripping him tightly. He lifted his mouth from hers and nipped her lip. She gasped, the sound ragged in the confines of the small space.

He guided her head back as his lips and tongue trailed along her jaw and down her neck. "Bloody cravat," he murmured.

Oh, how she wished she was wearing a gown!

But then it didn't matter what she was wearing at all because the hack drew to a startling and bitterly disappointing stop.

Jack eased back, his breaths filling the coach and indicating the pace of his heart matched her own. "I beg your forgiveness."

She felt the delicious heat in her core and looked him in the eye. "Absolutely not. I refuse to grant it."

He seemed to be at a loss for words, but quickly

recovered. "Keep your head down when you get out. Should I come with you?"

Yes, come with me. Stay with me.

"No. I'll see you—" She picked up her hat from the floor. "When will I see you?"

"Soon."

"We should visit Hodges."

"Yes." Maybe he really wasn't able to speak at the moment.

"Tomorrow?"

He shook his head. "Wednesday. No, Thursday. Two o'clock."

"Will you be on time?"

The driver knocked on the roof.

Jack opened the door, smiling. "Saucy wench."

She kissed him once more, fast and hard, her teeth drawing on his lower lip as she backed away. "Good night."

The smile on her face didn't fade as she made her way home, nor did it disappear when she fell asleep. In fact, it was still there when she awoke the next morning.

CHAPTER 9

The last two days had been the longest Viola could remember. Apparently, she missed seeing Jack Barrett.

And it hadn't even really been two days. Yet. But it would be longer than two days when she finally saw him tomorrow.

Oh, this simply wouldn't do. Neither would tossing restlessly at night as she relived his mouth on hers, his hands on her body... Even now as she sat in the library with Grandmama, peering at a map as she liked to do, she began to feel overheated.

Blenheim came into the library. "His Grace, the Duke of Eastleigh."

Val strode inside, a lock of blond hair grazing his forehead as it was often wont to do when he raked his hand through his hair. Or perhaps it had come dislodged from the style when he'd removed his hat. Whatever the reason, it never failed to give him a boyish charm that reminded Viola of their youth. Though they were five years apart, they had always been quite close, save the years he'd abandoned her to go to Oxford. Then, when he'd returned, she and Grandmama had moved to this house in Berkeley Square.

"How lovely to see you," Grandmama said, peering at him over the top of the glasses she wore to read. "I'd begun to think you forgot we existed."

"That's a bit of an exaggeration," Val said with a smile. "But I am newly married, and I have been doting upon my wife. Since this is a state you heartily desired, I would expect your understanding, if not wholehearted support."

Grandmama chuckled, displaying a rare flash of humor. "You are a devil. Just like your father. And your grandfather."

"Given the esteem you hold them both in, I shall take that as a very high compliment indeed." Val walked toward Viola where she sat at a table with her new map spread out in front of her. "What far-off places are you perusing today?"

"South America. I only purchased it yesterday. I'm fascinated by the Andes Mountains. Wouldn't you love to encounter mountains so tall you can't even see the tops some days because of the clouds?"

"She would much rather spend her time engrossed in such nonsense than do something productive," Grandmama said, immediately putting Viola on the defensive. The dowager was still annoyed with Viola for dancing with only one gentleman at the Goodrick ball last Saturday. Was it her fault only one gentleman had asked?

Two, really, but she didn't count Barrett because she hadn't danced with him. She'd actually wanted to, however not as much as she'd wanted to talk to him.

"Grandmama, when—and if—Viola decides to wed, it will be magnificent and for all the right and wonderful reasons," Val said cheerily. Spoken like a man who'd avoided the parson's trap until the perfect woman, the woman he adored, had come along.

Viola did not expect such fortune to strike her, not when it had smiled upon her brother. The odds were surely against her. Furthermore, she doubted such a man even existed. Her expectations were far too unreasonable for any man to consider.

Despite that very rational thought process, Jack Barrett rose in her mind. *Pooh.*

"It is precisely because of your happiness that Viola should open her mind to marriage." Grandmama sent her a disgruntled glower.

"Give her time," Val said softly.

"I've given her five long years," Grandmama said. "Are you prepared to care for your sister when I am gone?"

"Of course. I would never abandon Viola." Val gave her a smile of encouragement. "I shall provide whatever support she requires."

"Yes, but at what cost to your own family?" Grandmama scoffed and set her book down on the table to her right. She removed her glasses and deposited them atop the tome. "Help me up."

Val rushed to her aid, offering his hand and then clasping her elbow until she was steady on her feet.

Grandmama frowned up at him. "I'm not infirm." Then she strode from the library, her head high, her back as straight and stiff as a pole flying the Union Jack.

Viola groaned softly and laid her forehead against the map for a brief moment.

"Don't let her bother you," Val said, and given the sound of his voice, he'd come closer.

She lifted her head and saw that he stood next to the table. "I try not to, but it's becoming more difficult. Scarcely a day passes when she doesn't broach the subject."

"You know, it's not a terrible thing—"

"*Et tu, Brute?*"

"Love is wonderful. You should give it a chance."

She hadn't ever experienced it—not romantically,

anyway. "I am still a pariah. It's difficult to dance or converse with gentlemen when they don't approach you."

"Some do," he argued. "Didn't I see you with Jack Barrett at the Goodrick ball?"

Grandmama had seen her too and had, of course, commented on the fact that Viola had promenaded with him *twice* in one day. It was nearly a scandal! Or so Grandmama had said.

"We share common views on politics. Please don't suggest I shouldn't speak with him."

"I presume Grandmama has done that."

Viola adopted the dowager's imperious tone. "He's not the sort of gentleman I should wed."

Val grinned. "Did you tell her not to worry about it since he has no desire to marry? Jack is perhaps even more of a committed bachelor than I was. At least for now. He doesn't even take time for a mistress." He shot her a look of apology. "Forget I said that."

"I'm not a nun," Viola said, ignoring the spark of pleasure her brother's comment had provoked. No, she wasn't a nun, as evidenced by her kissing Jack the other night. And the fact that she was quite eager to do it again. Being attracted to him, however, was not love, and marriage to him—or anyone else—was out of the question.

Val pulled a letter from his coat. "This arrived for you at the Wicked Duke today."

She took the missive from him. Tavistock was marked across the front in large letters. Looking up at him, she lifted a shoulder as she opened it. As she directed her gaze toward the parchment, her pulse picked up with each word, and by the time she reached the end, she feared Val would see her chest rising and falling in distress.

Dear Mr. Tavistock,

Your inquiries into the matter involving the Prince Regent are proof the truth behind the attack must be made public. Mr. Jack Barrett, MP for Middlesex, is a known radical sympathizer and has been seen consorting with radical groups. He was seen meeting with one at the Crown and Anchor the evening before the attack on the Prince. Someone in that group has said Barrett organized the attack.

We believe you must publicize this information before another attack is launched.

Sincerely,

A concerned citizen

Viola's hands shook. Jack could not have done such a thing. It was impossible. He was trying to help her find out what had happened.

Was he, really?

He'd tried to convince her to stop the investigation. The other night at Brooks's, he steered her from the club before she'd had a chance to speak with anyone beyond Pennington. It was as if he was trying to control the inquiry. Which made sense if he was to blame.

Viola felt ill.

"What's that about?" Val asked.

She quickly folded the missive and set it in her lap. "Someone suggesting I write about them." Plenty of men at the Wicked Duke had tried to get her to do that.

Val chuckled. "I suppose some people like notoriety. Just keep me out of your column."

"I always do. Though I plan to mention your marriage and how blissful you seem. I'm afraid I can't help myself."

A laugh spilled from Val's lips, and he nodded. "I suppose there's no harm in that. In truth, there's never any harm in your column—you are universally kind when you write about others."

She thought of what could happen to the MP when she wrote about him. Only he wasn't just a nameless MP anymore. He was Jack Barrett, if the letter in her lap were to be believed. "I will be there tonight." She had to go. It was the best opportunity for her to see Jack. And she *had* to see him.

"I'll stop in later," he said. "See you then." He bent down and bussed her cheek, then departed.

Viola unfolded the letter and read it again. And again. After the fifth time, she had it committed to memory. Gone was her shock and dismay, replaced by anger and a sense of absolute betrayal.

Reason told her there was a chance this wasn't true. Was it reason? Or was it something far more foolish, such as the way she felt about him?

And how was that? She'd already determined love was out of the question, that she was merely attracted to Jack. That was an inconvenience she could —and would—overlook. She had to because she was in pursuit of the truth.

Right now, he was the primary obstacle in her way.

~

*J*ack trudged into the Wicked Duke at nearly ten. Bone weary after a day of debates, he probably should have gone home. Instead, he'd talked himself into stopping for an ale. The tavern was, sort of, on his way to King Street.

"Barrett!"

He raised his hand in greeting and was about to sit down in his usual spot when his gaze connected with that of Viola, rather, Tavistock. She sat in the corner with a few other men and was clearly aware of the moment he'd walked inside. Her eyes were glued to him, her jaw tense.

Something was wrong.

Mary handed him a mug of ale. "Good evening," she said. She batted her eyelashes and managed to graze his arm with her breast as she moved past him.

Frowning, he pushed her from his mind and looked back to Viola, who was still watching him. He inclined his head toward the rear of the tavern, hoping she would understand to meet him in the storage room.

He went into the private salon and casually made his way to the closet where he'd fixed Viola's side-burns last week. Inside the tiny room, he set his tankard on a shelf.

A few moments later, she came inside, closing the door behind her.

Being alone with her in the close, dimly lit space, he was catapulted back to the hack the other night when they'd kissed. Heat and desire pulsed through him, and he wondered if he'd maybe misread that anything was wrong. Perhaps she was as eager to kiss him again as he was her.

He moved toward her—it took only a step—and she flattened herself against the door. Reaching into her coat, she pulled out a folded piece of parchment, which she handed to him.

"Explain this, please," she said shortly. "If you can."

Unease crept across his shoulders as he took the paper. Moving to the small lantern affixed to the wall and its meager light, he held up the letter and read. Anger and incredulity warred in his brain.

Dropping the letter to his side, he turned to face her. "This isn't true."

"You weren't at that meeting at the Crown and Anchor?"

"I—" Dammit. "I was. Not at a meeting, but I was at the Crown and Anchor that night. It's a meeting place for a variety of reasons. I certainly wasn't there to orchestrate a plot to kill the prince."

"Then how do you explain this letter?"

He glanced down at the paper in his hand. "The rantings of a lunatic? Or a coward? The author didn't even sign his name. Clearly, someone wants to implicate me in the attack."

"You think someone wants me to write a story saying you instigated the attack on the prince?"

Who would do that? Many people, unfortunately. He had plenty of political enemies. But to think that any of them would go to these lengths made him sick. And angry.

"I can't think of any other explanation," he said quietly.

"Is it possible this person is mistaken? They saw you at the Crown and Anchor and assumed you were the MP who organized the attack?"

"Who's to say there was ever an MP involved at all?" If the closet weren't so damn small, he would have paced. "Perhaps the whole thing is a fabrication. Was there ever an MP who worked with the radicals, or was this simply an enterprise to discredit me?"

"Discredit you?" She stared at him. "This would see you imprisoned."

Probably—at least in the current climate. "There is no actual evidence," he said, hating that she'd doubted him. "There would be no conviction because *I haven't done anything.*"

He crumpled the edge of the letter in his grip as fury raged through him. When he found the person behind this... He lifted his gaze to hers. She was still pressed against the door, her blue eyes wary.

"You don't believe me." His tone was flat, his emotions deflating until he wasn't sure he felt anything.

"I...want to. I don't know what to believe. You are somewhat radical in your beliefs."

"As are you. Would you attempt to kill the Prince Regent? Perhaps I should ask what you were doing on that evening in January."

She sucked in a breath, and he immediately regretted what he'd said.

"I know you didn't have anything to do with it," he whispered. "I just wish you thought the same of me."

It was a long moment before she exhaled and responded. "You've repeatedly told me to be careful. I'm trying to be careful."

He could understand that. He looked at her intently, moving toward her, but not getting too close. "Then I'll prove my innocence to you. We'll go to the Crown and Anchor, and I'll introduce you to the men I met that night so they can tell you what we discussed."

Her gaze flickered with surprise. "Are they radicals?"

"They're Spencean Philanthropists. We discussed the upcoming trials of the men arrested for the Spa Fields riots. A friend of mine is defending one of them."

Her eyes widened, and her lips parted. "Oh." She tipped her head to the side. "Did you ask them about the attack? Perhaps they know what really happened."

"No, I didn't." He could almost hear her outrage.

"As a reporter, it is my duty to follow wherever my inquiries lead. You withheld pertinent information from me."

He had anger of his own—she didn't understand the danger of the situation. "I was trying to protect you. They are a radical organization, Viola. Some of them are in prison awaiting trial for *treason*."

Her eyes narrowed. "You are not responsible for protecting me. You are not my brother nor are you my husband." Her tone was a devastating mixture of furious heat and derisive cold.

They stood there staring at each other a moment. He handed the letter back to her. "Tomorrow, we'll go to the Crown and Anchor instead of the coffeehouse."

She visibly relaxed, her jaw loosening and her shoulders dropping. "Should we go in the evening?"

He shook his head. That would be infinitely more dangerous. "Same time we'd planned to meet at the coffeehouse. I'll make the arrangements. And I'll pick you up in a hack at the edge of Berkeley Square."

She nodded, then finally pushed away from the door. This brought them closer than they'd been the entire time they'd been in the closet.

The idea that she'd wanted to get him alone to kiss him again seemed woefully ludicrous now. The other night in the hack had been a wild, singular event. He had to stop hoping it would happen again.

He reached for the door, and she moved to the side. "See you tomorrow."

She nodded but didn't respond. Jack left and hoped tomorrow wouldn't be a mistake.

CHAPTER 10

The Crown and Anchor was a sizeable tavern just off the Strand on Arundel Street. Like the Wicked Duke, all manner of men met here. Unlike the Wicked Duke, the Crown and Anchor had space for large formal meetings. Jack led Viola inside to the main parlor.

She tipped her head back and looked up at the coffered ceiling with its decorative woodwork and the pair of chandeliers decorating the room. "Is it true Charles James Fox celebrated a birthday here once?" she asked.

He nodded. "Yes, there were over two thousand people, apparently. Twenty-some years ago, this was the primary meeting location for the London Corresponding Society."

"Weren't they also a radical group?"

"Right again. Their activities prompted the passage of antisedition laws, which have been recently and unfortunately resurrected."

She continued to study the room. "Can you imagine if the Wicked Duke had interiors such as this?"

"No, but then I find the Wicked Duke quite comfortable."

"I do too, which is strange since I'm a woman and most of the patrons are men." She added, "There *are* women there, mostly staff, but I daresay you are quite aware."

There was an odd quality to her tone that drew his attention. "Why do you say that?"

"Mary flirts with you."

He led her farther inside, looking about the room to locate the Spenceans. "The barmaid? She's friendly, I suppose."

"She practically throws herself at you. How can you not be aware of that?"

"Yes, I'm aware. I just decide not to engage her—or her designs. It's better to just ignore them."

She stared at him and shook her head slightly. "Men are so bizarre. One would think after two years masquerading as one, I would understand you better."

Was she jealous? "I have no interest in Mary, and I never have." He hoped she understood what he meant, that he'd never touched—or kissed—Mary. "I have little time for romantic entanglements. None, really."

"I see." The odd tone had disappeared, and if Jack had to describe her expression, he would have said it was smug. He quashed a chuckle in response. "So these Spenceans just sit out in the open?" she asked quietly.

"There are only a few, and there's no law against that number coming together."

"It's any meeting over fifty," she said. "Correct?"

He nodded as he recognized Henry Dean and led her to a table on the other side of the room beneath a wide painting of boats on the River Thames. "Good afternoon, Dean. Allow me to introduce my friend Tavistock."

Dean stood and offered his hand to Viola. She

gripped it firmly, demonstrating a strong, masculine handshake. She might not think like a man, but she'd worked hard to master the outward appearance.

"Pleased to meet you, Tavistock. You both need beer." Dean, a burly man in his forties missing a little finger, waved his hand.

Jack and Viola were barely seated before the ale was delivered in two tankards. "Thank you for meeting with us today," Viola said.

Dean nodded as he sipped his ale. Setting the tankard down, he glanced between Jack and Viola. "How can I help you?"

Jack had sent him a note requesting the meeting and had only said they needed help with something. "It's a sensitive issue."

"I presume it's to do with the Spenceans." His deep voice reverberated across the table even though he'd lowered his volume. "Everything about that is sensitive."

Jack exchanged a look with Viola, then plowed forward. "It's come to our attention that someone in the group may have worked to agitate things after Spa Fields."

"No one had to work at it," Dean said. "We were all agitated after that."

"Agitated enough to try to assassinate the prince?" Jack asked.

Dean's amber eyes widened briefly. "Careful what you say there, Barrett."

"It's not an accusation at all. You know my feelings toward your organization." He supported their ideas if not the vitriol of some of the members. He hated that they were being silenced. "Someone is trying to tie *me* to the attack. Someone is putting it out that I was here at a meeting the night before."

"Bloody hell," Dean breathed. "You were here, but

it was just you and I and a few other men discussing Watson and the others."

Jack turned his head to Viola briefly. "Watson was one of those arrested in the Spa Fields riot."

She nodded in response, then swung her gaze across the table to Dean. "Can you think of anyone who might have been here? Someone who would have seen Barrett and would want to link him to the attack?"

Dean frowned and stared into his tankard for a moment. When he looked up, his gaze was pensive. "I can't think of anyone, but this is a large place. No one I know would seek to make trouble for Barrett." He nodded toward Jack. "As long as I've known you, you've preached nonviolent protest and open dialogue."

While that was good to hear, it didn't bring them any closer to finding answers. "I'm glad to know you feel that way, but you can see why I'm trying to find the truth."

Dean stroked his chin. "If it was a Spencean—and I don't think it was—he acted alone. We didn't coordinate anything."

"I assumed as much," Jack said. "Did any new members join late last year? Anyone behave in a manner that would suggest they might commit an act of violence?"

Dean shook his head. "I'm sorry I can't help you. We're rather scattered since Spa Fields. Our leaders are in prison."

Four of them were awaiting trial. "I understand." Jack picked up his ale and took a long draught to ease his frustration.

"When is your next meeting?" Viola asked.

Jack set his tankard down as dread curled through him. She wanted to go to a meeting. Did she have any idea how dangerous that was right now? He couldn't let her go, and she was going to be furious with him.

"We aren't really having meetings," Dean said slowly, his eyes wary as he regarded Viola.

"Tavistock isn't going to inform anyone of your meetings—whether you have them or not. *If* you are having one, it might be helpful if I could attend."

Dean blinked at him in surprise. "You'd endanger yourself? You need to be careful right now, Barrett."

"We all do," Jack said darkly. "But I also need to clear my name before someone tries to have me arrested."

Dean pressed his mouth into a grim line. "The fourteenth at the Bull and Fox."

"I know it well." The small tavern was situated near Lincoln's Inn Fields. Jack had spent plenty of time there when he'd studied the law. "Later in the evening?"

Dean nodded before taking another drink of ale. "There's always a chance we don't do it—we won't endanger anyone."

"Understood." Jack looked over at Viola to silently communicate it was time to go.

"Will you be there?" Dean asked Viola.

"Er, no. I have another engagement that evening. My apologies."

Jack lifted his tankard higher to mask his surprise, then swallowed another gulp of beer. He was more than shocked. He was impressed.

"Just as well," Dean said. "Many of the men know Jack and won't mind him being there, but you're a stranger. That would make a few of them nervous."

"I wouldn't want to do that," Viola said.

Dean inclined his head toward her. "You're a good friend to help Barrett with his inquiries."

That had been the reason Jack had provided as to why there would be an unknown gentleman at their meeting today. "I need all the friends I can get right now," Jack said, standing.

Viola got to her feet, and Dean did the same. He reached across the table and shook Jack's hand. "You've a friend here too."

"I appreciate it, Dean." Jack gripped his hand, then let go.

A moment later, Jack and Viola walked out onto the Strand. It took only a moment for him to hail a hack. He looked over at her. "Do you mind if I get out at Charing Cross? I need to get back to Westminster." He felt strange letting her continue alone to Berkeley Square, but reasoned she'd been carrying on as Tavistock by herself for some time.

"Not at all. I'm quite capable of seeing myself home."

"I wasn't sure—it is broad daylight, after all. Not your usual time to be out." He winked at her to show he was teasing. He gave the driver their directions and climbed into the hack after her.

This was a larger vehicle than the one they'd taken last time, and he was able to sit across from her, which was perhaps for the best. The more distance between them, the less he was drawn to her. Or so he'd tell himself.

He scrutinized her across the interior. "Do you really have an engagement on the fourteenth?"

"No."

"I'm surprised you don't want to attend the meeting."

A smile teased her lips, and it was very hard to see Tavistock and not Viola. "I *do* want to attend, but I'm eager, not stupid. In all honesty, I'm not even sure I want you to go."

A hint of joy flitted through him. She cared about him. And he cared about her. Their association had transformed into something he'd never expected.

"I have to go," he said. "I must find out who is trying to make it look as if I had something to do with the attack."

She looked at him intently. "Who are your enemies?"

"I wouldn't say I had 'enemies.' I disagree with plenty of other MPs, but there's a professional courtesy and trust. At least I thought there was." He didn't bother hiding his disgust. He couldn't imagine who would go to such lengths. "I'm apparently a bit naïve," he said.

"I don't think so. This is beyond the pale." She didn't bother disguising her dismay either.

They were quiet a moment, then she said, "I'm sorry I doubted you. I understand why you didn't tell me about meeting with the Spenceans and why you didn't take me to meet them. I comprehended that it's a dangerous time, but perhaps not as fully as I should have. I do now."

He smiled across the hack at her. "Good. It was never my intent to keep things from you."

The hack started to slow and pull to the side of the road. Jack looked out to see they were nearly at Charing Cross.

"I suppose I won't talk to you until after the fourteenth?" she asked as the hack came to a stop.

"Probably not." He hoped he didn't sound as disappointed as he felt.

"Please be careful. I would hate to see you in prison."

"I would hate that too." He laughed, then climbed out of the hack.

He stood on the curb and watched the vehicle reenter traffic while he mentally counted four, no *five*, days before he would see her again. It felt like an eternity.

Hell.

For the first time in his life, Jack was utterly captivated, and he didn't have the slightest idea what to do about it.

~

*V*iola hoped Grandmama appreciated that she'd danced. With a viscount.

She held Lord Orford's arm as they left the dance floor. "Thank you for the dance, my lord," she said politely.

"It was my pleasure. I am only sorry I wasn't able to attend the Goodrick ball last week as intended. I regretted not fulfilling my promise to dance with you." It hadn't been a *promise*, but she supposed it was nice of him to remember. "Might we promenade for a few moments?"

"Certainly." She was eager to continue their conversation from the park and wasn't sure they'd be able to. The quadrille they'd just danced hadn't lent itself to much in the way of conversation and certainly nothing so weighty as the assassination attempt on the Prince Regent.

She launched right into the topic lest she lose the opportunity. "I hope you don't find me impertinent, but I wished to ask about our discussion last week in the park. It seems as if you perhaps knew something about that...attack." She chose her words carefully and kept her voice low as they circuited the ballroom, passing countless people. She registered many familiar faces, but none of them belonged to Jack Barrett.

And that was how she knew she'd been looking for him.

"Lady Viola, it seemed as if *you* knew something about the...incident," Orford said in a measured tone.

"I do not."

"Alas, I do not either." He paused and looked down at her. "This is a rather dangerous topic, and you've brought it up twice now, which I find a trifle peculiar."

Blast. Perhaps she wasn't a very good reporter at all. "I heard a piece of gossip, 'tis all." She spoke lightly and looked out over the ballroom.

They continued walking. "You should know not to listen to gossip." His tone was condescendingly parental.

She fluttered her eyelashes at him in mock innocence. "Even you can recognize that gossip about such a thing would be intriguing. Or do you not care for the welfare of our prince?"

He sputtered for a moment. "Of course I care. That you would insinuate otherwise is, frankly, insulting."

"I didn't insinuate a thing, Lord Orford," she said sweetly. "I asked you a question, and I'm glad to hear you admire the prince as much as I do." Admiration was perhaps a shade excessive—the man was a hedonist and not a very good husband—but in this instance, it seemed the best thing to say.

Lord Orford opened his mouth to speak, then snapped it closed again. She suspected he wanted to ask what she'd heard, but to do so would encourage gossip, which he'd just denigrated. He'd pompoused himself into a corner, and Viola had to stifle a smile.

Thankfully, they'd arrived at her grandmother, who was seated in a chair against the wall. Her friend, the Dowager Countess of Dunwich, was no longer occupying the seat next to her.

Grandmama looked up at Viola and Lord Orford. "You looked quite lovely dancing. I trust you enjoyed yourselves?"

Viola withdrew her hand from his arm. "We did, thank you."

Lord Orford bowed to the dowager and then to Viola. "Have a good evening."

Perching on the empty chair beside Grandmama, Viola mentally bid the viscount good riddance.

"He would be a good match," Grandmama said.

"So you've indicated. However, I find him arrogant."

"All men are arrogant." Grandmama's tone was dismissive. "The sooner you accept that, the sooner you can settle on someone. You said the same thing of Ledbury."

Perhaps Grandmama was right, though she would argue there was an arrogance scale. She'd place Ledbury somewhere below Orford, but far above her brother or Jack. The two of them were also arrogant, but not in a way that annoyed her. How did that work exactly? Their brand of arrogance was more confidence and self-awareness. Perhaps she ought to write an article about the arrogance of men...

"Viola!"

She snapped out of her reverie and blinked at her grandmother. "What?"

"I said there is a man for you. You just haven't identified him yet."

Viola wasn't sure she believed that. She'd met an endless parade of men in the past seven years. What if she were doomed to be alone?

Doomed? Since when had the notion of being alone ever bothered her?

"What if I don't...identify anyone?" she asked softly, not meeting Grandmama's gaze.

"Nonsense. Mildred is back."

Viola looked up to see Lady Dunwich. She stood, offering the woman, who was a few years Grandmama's senior and walked with a cane, the chair.

"Did you have a nice dance, dear?" Lady Dunwich asked brightly. Her friendship with Grandmama had always puzzled Viola. Where Grandmama was austere and sometimes terrifying, Lady Dunwich was warm and charming. Yet they were as close as two friends could be. "Lord Orford is so very handsome." She gave Viola a knowing glance.

"Yes, we had a nice dance." Viola refused to acknowledge whether he was handsome. While he possessed an attractive form, he paled beside Jack, whose sparkling intellect and vibrant charm made him wholly alluring. Along with that arrogance or confidence or whatever it was. She caught herself scanning the ballroom for him again. Instead of finding him, she saw Isabelle and decided she'd rather talk to her than remain and discuss Lord Orford.

"Will you excuse me? I'm going to speak with Isabelle." She curtsied to Lady Dunwich and inclined her head toward Grandmama, then took herself off with alacrity.

Isabelle greeted her warmly. "What a fetching gown," she said, looking down at Viola's dark green dress embellished with gold embroidery.

"Thank you. It's earned me two dances tonight, which is a record since before Ledbury."

"That's cause for celebration. Shall we have champagne?" Isabelle frowned. "*Is* it cause for celebration? You don't seem very enthusiastic. In fact, you looked slightly panicked as you made your way over here."

Panicked? "Grandmama was pressing Orford as a possible match, but I find him condescending."

"Then scratch him off the list."

She gave Isabelle a sardonic look. "There is no list."

"Do you want there to be?"

The word "no" burned her tongue, and yet she couldn't force it from her mouth. The panic Isabelle had recognized seized control of her so that she was utterly frozen. Maybe she did want a list. Or at least a list of one. Because all it took was one. One man to fall in love with and to fall in love with her. But the idea that two people could find each other and that magic would happen seemed completely impossible. Except she had only to look at Isabelle—and Val—to know that wasn't true.

Maybe it just wasn't true for Viola.

Not only was she a pariah, she liked to study maps and write until her fingers turned black from the ink. She hated dancing—mostly—and she liked to discuss politics. What if no man would ever find her attractive enough, and not just physically, to want to marry her? Had she unconsciously made herself undesirable to avoid marriage? The better question was why would she want to *stop* avoiding marriage? What was going *on*?

Feeling as though her world was tipping on its axis, she sought to escape. "Excuse me while I go to the retiring room," she murmured.

She turned and made her way from the ballroom in a blur. The retiring room was upstairs, she thought, but before she reached the stairs, she saw the one man she'd been searching for all evening. The one man who was, at least, attracted to her physically. Or had been once. Maybe.

Viola rushed forward and grabbed his hand. Wordlessly, she looked around for a place to go. Past the stairs was a slender door that looked like it might lead to a closet.

She opened the door and exhaled with relief—yes, a closet. Then she pulled him inside and closed them into darkness.

"Viola?" Jack asked, sounding very confused.

"Am I unlovable?" she blurted.

"Are you—" He drew in an audible breath. "I am not the best person to ask. Because I've never been in love," he added quickly.

"Neither have I." She still held his hand, which was how she knew where he was in orientation to her. The closet was smaller than the one they'd visited at the Wicked Duke, and it smelled of linen and soap instead of hops and barley.

"Perhaps we're both unlovable," she said.

"I don't think—"

She didn't want to think either, so instead of letting him finish, she tugged on his hand. "Just be quiet and kiss me."

His chest crashed softly into hers as his hand snaked around her waist and held her against him. His mouth found her cheek, and she would never know if that was intentional or not—nor would she ever care. He kissed her repeatedly, traversing her flesh until he found her lips, and then heat exploded between them.

Viola clutched at his shoulders and held on tightly as he wrapped her in his arms. Their tongues met with wild abandon, and she clasped the sides of his neck, tucking her fingers beneath his collar and cravat to feel the warmth of his skin.

He angled his head and deepened the kiss, exploring her while she did the same. She wanted more of this, more of him. She wanted *all* of him.

His hand pressed against her lower back, bringing their pelvises together. Despite the layers of her petticoat and gown, she felt the faint steel of his erection, and need bloomed between her legs.

He pulled away with a soft groan but didn't leave her. His lips trailed across her jaw and down her neck. "We should stop now," he murmured against her even as his tongue traced across her collarbone.

Yes, they should, but she couldn't. Not yet.

Viola moaned and clutched at his head, wishing they could tear their clothes away. *Yes.* She longed to strip him naked and see the hard planes of his chest and the delicious curve of his backside.

Good Lord, she was a wanton. And she didn't care one bit.

He inhaled against her flesh. "You smell so good." His mouth closed over her skin just above the top of her gown, and the moment she gasped, he tore his lips away.

"We should stop," he repeated before claiming her mouth once more.

The kiss was frenzied and hot, wet tongues parrying while hands searched for new places to explore. He cupped the underside of her breast as she gripped his hip and dared to cup his backside.

Finally, they pulled apart, panting. "We should stop." This time, he sounded as though he meant it.

She couldn't disagree. It wasn't as if she could lose her virginity in the closet of the—where were they again?—whoever's town house. "We should." The words did not convince her body, however. Her core pulsed with need while her breasts tingled, and her fingers itched to touch him.

"I was on my way to the retiring room," she offered rather lamely.

"I've only just arrived. I'd hoped to see you."

"And so you have." She tried to laugh, but it came out sounding fake.

"Only for a second. I can't actually see you at all in here, which is a crying shame since you look like Viola instead of Tavistock." He sounded disappointed.

"Oh." She was momentarily at a loss for words. "You prefer me as Viola?"

"I prefer you with breasts, which I could definitely feel." His voice was now dark and strained. "This is not a good direction of conversation. You should go."

"All right. It was nice to see you. Or not see you, I mean."

"It was...*spectacular*," he said, heating every part of her that wasn't already on fire for him. Which wasn't anything, she realized, so really, he'd just increased the fervor with which she wanted him.

She wanted him?

Oh, yes.

"I'm going now." Despite the unsatisfied lust coursing through her, her pulse had slowed to a degree that she felt she could step out of the closet without looking as if she'd been nearly ravished.

With great reluctance, she found the latch and let herself out of the closet. Then she dashed up the stairs to the retiring room and prayed it was empty.

It wasn't, of course, but fortune was smiling upon her, for the only person present was Isabelle. Who was looking at Viola with a mix of expectation and concern. Viola realized she'd left the ballroom first to come here. Now Isabelle was here, and she'd arrived before Viola...

"I was waylaid by a...friend," Viola said, thinking the excuse sounded stupid. Probably because it was.

"A dark-haired gentleman friend?" Isabelle asked softly. Then her mouth ticked up in a smile before she quickly quashed it. "I saw you go into the closet with him—I'd followed you out of the ballroom because you seemed upset. Now, however, you seem... Never mind."

Alarm speared through Viola. "You saw us?"

Isabelle nodded. "I don't think anyone else did. I checked the corridor. Still, I could have been anyone."

"Yes." Viola ought to be horrified—and she was—but not enough to regret a moment.

"Don't worry, I won't tell anyone. I am not about to begrudge you...whatever it was you were doing, but please be careful."

Viola laughed. "Why, because of my reputation? It scarcely matters. I know Grandmama wants me to wed, but the fact remains that I am hardly marriageable as far as most men are concerned." Which had always suited her fine. But for the first time, she wasn't so sure.

"Do you really believe that's true? Lord Orford didn't seem to think so. Why else would he dance with you?" Isabelle asked.

"Because he's an idiot?" Viola was far more comfortable trying to find humor in the situation. If she didn't, she'd have to think about it too closely, and she was rather afraid of what she might find.

She feared she'd find she did care about her reputation. That she really was unlovable—not even Jack had been able to confirm she wasn't. And worst of all, that she wanted to find a husband. That she wanted someone to love her.

Because maybe *she* was falling in love with someone.

No. She absolutely refused to consider it.

CHAPTER 11

*T*he Bull and Fox was a small tavern tucked just outside Lincoln's Inn Fields. It was a popular meeting place for law students and young solicitors, as well as the occasional radical. There was a small meeting room upstairs where people debated the law and politics, and that was where tonight's clandestine meeting of the Spencean Philanthropists was taking place.

If it was taking place.

Jack made his way up the narrow stairs and rapped softly on the door. Henry Dean opened it a bare amount and, upon seeing Jack, invited him inside.

There were perhaps twenty men in attendance. Burly working men and artisans like Dean. Jack recognized a few, but not all. Dean introduced Jack as John Barr, which was his actual first name and half of his surname, and Jack went around shaking hands. He ended up seated beside a whitesmith named John Castle. The meeting began, and they discussed the imprisonment of their leaders, with Dean giving an update on their legal defense.

Jack knew the barristers working on the cases and believed the men were in as good hands as they could hope. After that, they discussed the Manchester march and then lamented the departure of William Cobbett—a radical hero.

"The *Political Register* lives on, thanks to Benbow," Dean said. Cobbett's newspaper was widely read by the working class, a fact that annoyed many of Jack's colleagues in Parliament.

Finally, the meeting concluded, and conversation sprang up around the room. Jack decided to start in with Castle and turned to the man beside him. "I think I might have seen you at a meeting before."

Castle shrugged. "It's possible. I've been coming for a couple of years now."

"Were you at Spa Fields?"

He chuckled. "If you don't know, I won't say."

Jack supposed that was the best answer—at least the safest one. But it didn't give him much optimism at getting to the truth tonight. "What about the day Parliament opened. Were you there outside?"

Castle's eyes narrowed. "Are you referring to the attack on Prinny? You'd best not be accusing me of anything."

"I am not. I was hoping someone had seen something. Do you know if anyone did?"

"Wouldn't say if I did," Castle said firmly.

Jack's frustration grew. "I don't wish to get anyone in trouble. I'm only trying to—never mind." He stood up and started toward the door.

Dean met him before he could leave. "What's the matter?"

"It was a mistake to come here. I can't expect these men to trust me, and I don't know how they can help me. Someone out there is spreading rumors and lies about me, and I don't even know where to begin."

"Who are your enemies?"

"Someone else asked me the same question."

Viola rose in his mind, and with it, a burst of longing so strong, it stole his breath. "I didn't think I had any—at least not anyone who would link me with an assassination attempt—but clearly, I was wrong." Perhaps he was going about this in a convoluted way. Perhaps he should spend his energy every day trying to determine who truly *was* his enemy, who would want to cause him harm in this way. "I'm not even entirely sure of this person's—or people's —motive."

"Seems like that might be easy. You've been a champion for people like us, and that must make you unpopular in Parliament sometimes."

"Yes, but I am not alone in my endeavors."

"For all you know, others may be experiencing your same troubles."

That was an excellent point. Jack would speak with Burdett and others as soon as possible to ascertain whether they had encountered any difficulty such as he was.

"Thank you, Dean." Jack clapped him on the shoulder, thinking it hadn't been a mistake or waste of time to come here after all.

He left the tavern and caught a hack to take him home.

Being in a hack reminded him of Viola. Apparently, things people said also reminded him of Viola. Was there anything that didn't make him think of her?

Jack leaned his head back against the squab and closed his eyes, allowing his mind to wander where it wanted to go. To Viola. Specifically to kissing her in that closet the other night at the ball.

To have her—as Viola, not Tavistock—in his arms had been an unbelievable gift. He'd almost been unable to let go. What was happening to him?

He opened his eyes and scrubbed a hand over his

face. Was this what falling in love felt like? His father would know.

Jack thought of what his father had told him, about not waiting to marry. And yet Jack was committed to his professional path. When the Whigs regained power, he hoped to receive a government appointment. That meant dedicating his time and energy to Parliament, not a wife and family.

His father's anguish, which Jack had never known about, lingered in his mind. Regret was a terrible emotion.

What exactly was he trying to talk himself into?

Nothing. He couldn't fall in love with Viola. That would be madness for so many reasons. Even if he wanted to wed right now, she had no desire to do so, and that wasn't going to change in five years if Jack stuck to his marriage schedule.

There was no denying, however, that they were attracted to each other. Perhaps they could have an affair…

Jack straightened and rubbed his forehead as if he could massage the idiocy out of his brain. Was he really contemplating a liaison with a duke's sister? Scandal might be well and good for royal dukes, but Jack was simply an MP with cabinet aspirations. Not that any of that mattered—he couldn't sully Viola in such a way. Yes, she was an independent woman who forged her own path, but he'd already overstepped in ways he shouldn't have.

If he were a true gentleman, he'd cut ties with her completely. This investigation wasn't going anywhere, and could end up in disaster if they weren't careful.

Viola would be upset. She was absolutely committed to writing this article about the attack on the prince. What could she possibly write? Perhaps he could give her other information to write about—

topics from the House of Commons that she could distill into a weekly column. He'd ask her about it. Together, they could come up with something that would inspire and excite her.

But then they'd still be working as a team, and that contradicted what he needed to do.

Hell. He'd made a mess, and he feared untangling himself would only ensure things got even messier.

～

*I*t was a splendid afternoon for a ride or stroll in Hyde Park. It was the type of day and the time of the Season that brought the highest number of people out, and therefore it somewhat resembled a swarm of bees. Vehicles and horses jockeyed for position, and pedestrians hardly moved because they were constantly running into people they knew and stopping to converse.

Amidst all this, Viola tried to find Jack. For now, she sat in Grandmama's brougham as it traveled—slowly—around the Ring. His note had said to meet him here just after five o'clock, but now she wished they'd met earlier, before it had become such a crush.

After a quarter hour, she still didn't see him and sat back against the seat, feeling defeated. What if she never found him? She was dying to know what had transpired at the Spencean meeting.

At last, she caught sight of his familiar form striding along the footpath. She reached for the door. "Grandmama, I'm going to get out and take a walk."

The footman jumped down and opened the door before Viola could do so.

"I'm going to have Turner park in the shade," Grandmama said. "It's just a trifle too warm for me today."

"I'll look for you." Viola stepped down with the

footman's assistance and made her way to the foot-path. A butterfly flitted past her head, and she likened the fluttering of its wings to the giddiness in her belly.

Giddy at the prospect of seeing Jack.

He bowed when they met and offered her his arm so they could take a respectable promenade. In her mind, she was spiriting him off to a secluded grove where they could continue what they'd been doing in that closet at the ball...

"I'm pleased to see you are all right after last night's meeting," she said.

"I am, thank you. Overall, it was a pointless endeavor, I'm afraid."

She snapped her head toward him in distress. "Was it?"

He nodded grimly. "Who among that group would admit to me, an MP, that they'd been involved with the attack on the prince in some way? The moment I broached the subject, offense was taken, and rightly so, I suppose." He shook his head. "I am not an investigator, and I'm beginning to think we should leave that to Bow Street."

"Should we go to Bow Street?" she asked eagerly.

"And tell them what?"

She slowed. "We could show them the letter I received about you."

He stopped entirely. "You still have it?"

"It's securely locked away—I thought it was important to keep it as evidence."

"That's one way of looking at it, I suppose." His tone was wry. "It's also incriminating, don't you think?"

"Which is why it's safely hidden." She lowered her voice even more. "While I'd like to write a story about whatever happened, I think our primary goal right now should be ensuring your reputation."

His gaze locked with hers, the dark walnut of his eyes heating. "Viola, that is—"

She would never know what it was because they were interrupted at that very moment by the arrival of Mr. Caldwell and Sir Humphrey.

"Barrett, I've heard some distressing news," Caldwell said, his mouth forming something between a frown and a grimace. Sir Humphrey stood beside him, looking equally disturbed.

"Have you?" Jack's question was casually spoken, but Viola felt him tense.

"It's come to our attention you were seen at a meeting of the Spencean Philanthropists last night." Caldwell spoke so loudly that the people walking around them stopped and turned to stare at what was going on.

"Furthermore, it seems as though you had something to do with the Spa Fields riots and maybe even the ghastly attack on the Prince Regent."

Anger and fear prompted Viola to blurt, "That's absurd." She looked over at Jack, who barely seemed to register what he was being accused of, save the tightening of his mouth and jaw.

"Careful with your accusations," he said softly, almost menacingly. His tone made Viola's neck prickle.

Caldwell straightened, his gaze both taunting and superior. "You were seen at the Bull and Fox last night. Can you prove you weren't there?"

He could not. Because he *had* been there. Oh, this was an absolute disaster.

"I can," Viola said without thinking. She ignored the sudden clasp of Jack's hand over hers on his arm.

Sir Humphrey scoffed. "How can you do that?"

She glared at him and then at Caldwell for good measure. "Because he was with me."

"*Viola.*" The urgent whisper floated to her from Jack's lips.

Turning her head, she tried to use her eyes to silently plead with him to go along with what she was saying. If he contradicted her, he would only look even more guilty because she'd tried to hide the fact that he *had* been at the Bull and Fox.

Caldwell sneered. "You're saying Barrett couldn't have been at the Spencean meeting because he was with *you*? We're supposed to just believe that?"

Viola straightened her spine and gave him a haughty stare she was sure her grandmother would be proud of. Oh God, her grandmother... She couldn't think about her right now. "Yes. My brother is the Duke of Eastleigh. My testimony as to Mr. Barrett's whereabouts last night should be more than sufficient proof. I would also add that you'd better have evidence about his *alleged* participation in any radical events. Now, you will excuse us."

She pivoted and dragged Jack along with her. Searching wildly for Grandmama's brougham, she saw it parked beneath a tree on the other side of the Ring. "Hell," she muttered, quickening her pace. "We need to get to my grandmother."

"Where?"

"Over on the other side of the Ring."

They kept to the footpath, though she was tempted to cut across the grass to the other path that would take them to where Grandmama was parked.

"What on earth were you doing back there?" he sounded...angry.

"Why are you upset with me?" She worked to keep her focus straight ahead lest she become aware of anyone looking at them. It was too much to hope no one had overheard what had been said. But even if they hadn't, Caldwell and Sir Humphrey were likely telling anyone who would listen.

She'd just claimed—out loud, on the busiest after-noon of the Season in Hyde Park—that she'd been with Jack Barrett, MP, last night. In reality, she had been at home while Grandmama had attended a card party at Lady Dunwich's.

"I'm angry because you just created a massive scandal—for both of us."

"I'm not new at that," she said quietly.

"I am."

Viola flinched. The worst part of abandoning your betrothed at the altar was the fact that it hadn't just affected her, which she had been more than willing to endure. She'd known her reputation would be ruined and had hated that Ledbury's would be tainted. He'd survived, of course, and so had she. She would survive again. Would Jack?

She walked even faster as they turned to the other footpath that would take them to the brougham. Her mind scrambled to think of how to fix this for Jack. She didn't care about herself. She'd long ago accepted her pariah status. But Jack was a rising political star. Still, wasn't this better than being seen at a meeting of known radicals?

"I'm sorry," she said. "I wasn't thinking. I was just trying to protect you. We'll come up with something. Perhaps Val and Isabelle can say they were with us— we had dinner. And I didn't say all that because I was flustered. Yes, that could work."

"Assuming they weren't somewhere else last night that would completely destroy your fake alibi." He blew out a frustrated breath. "While I appreciate you wanting to protect me, you shouldn't have said any-thing. I haven't done anything wrong. It's not a crime to be somewhere."

"No, but it could be incredibly damaging."

"So can this." His tone was dark, and he was clearly not done being angry.

They arrived at Grandmama's brougham, and it was immediately evident that she already knew. A group of people hurried away from the vehicle. Grandmama sat inside, her gaze icy as she stared at Viola. "Get in."

The footman helped Viola into the vehicle, and when she tried to sit beside her grandmother, Grandmama gestured to the rear-facing seat. "Sit over there. Where I can glower at you." She looked down at Jack. "When is the wedding?"

Jack returned her stare without wavering. "I will call on you tomorrow to discuss it."

"You will call on us right now."

"Grandmama, we aren't getting married," Viola said, hating the impassivity of Jack's expression. He was obviously angry, but was he anything else? She couldn't tell.

Viola expected her to argue, but Jack spoke first. "Yes, we are," he said firmly and without looking at Viola. He continued to stare at the dowager, then inclined his head before turning and walking toward the gate.

Was he going to Berkeley Square? Why didn't he just ride with them? She was about to suggest that, but her grandmother's furious expression quashed anything she'd considered saying.

"Drive," Grandmama said to Turner.

As they left the park, Viola finally summoned some words. "I wasn't really with him."

"It hardly matters. You said you were, and all of Mayfair has now heard it."

"Surely not *all* of Mayfair."

"Don't be cute with me, Viola. I am positively livid you would behave in this manner *again*. You seem to think you are immune, that somehow my influence will shield you from Society's judgment. It will not. It barely did the first time, and it surely won't now."

"I don't expect protection. I was trying to protect

him. Mr. Barrett. He was being accused of something he didn't do."

"So you made up a story about spending the evening with him?" Grandmama settled herself back against the seat. "Explain yourself."

Viola decided it was time to tell her the truth—about everything. Mostly everything. Some of the bits between her and Jack she would keep to herself. Not only did she not want to share it, she was confident Grandmama wouldn't want to hear it. As it was, she wouldn't like much of what Viola was about to reveal. "I suppose I should start at the very beginning."

"That would be a good place," Grandmama said testily.

"About two years ago, I began to dress as a man called Tavistock."

Grandmama's eyes nearly bulged from her head. "*You* are Tavistock? The columnist in the *Ladies' Gazette?*"

"It was the only way they would allow me to write for them. They don't hire women."

"To write for a woman's magazine?" Grandmama pursed her lips. "Idiots."

Viola tamped down a smile—now was not the time to indulge in humor. In the amount of time it took to drive to Berkeley Square, she'd explained about being Tavistock, about pursuing the story regarding the attack on the Prince Regent, and about working with Jack and how he was now the target of dangerous gossip and accusations.

"I see why you wanted to protect him, but it was foolishly done," Grandmama said as the brougham pulled to a stop in front of her house. "Actually, I don't see why you wanted to protect him. Are you in love with Mr. Barrett?"

"I— No." She'd been about to say she didn't know.

But she suspected she *did* know, and she preferred to pretend she didn't. So she'd lie to her grandmother and to herself.

When they were out of the brougham and walking to the house, Viola continued, "I had to protect him because he went to that meeting last night for me, to help with my story. I can't let him suffer for aiding me—he could end up in prison."

"Balderdash. He would never go to prison." Grandmama preceded her into the house. In the entrance hall, she paused to remove her hat and gloves, which she handed to Blenheim. Viola did the same. "Mr. Barrett will be calling shortly, Blenheim. Show him into the library."

Grandmama moved into the library, and Viola followed. When the dowager was situated in her favorite chair and Viola perched on a settee, her expression was much improved. She almost looked...pleased?

"No, Mr. Barrett would never go to prison. He's an important MP with a brilliant future, likely a title."

Viola began to understand Grandmama's transformation. Jack was now her favorite person in the world because he was about to do what no one had been able to do—secure Viola's hand in marriage. Only that wasn't going to happen. Just as with Ledbury, this marriage would never take place.

CHAPTER 12

*J*ack took his time walking to Berkeley Square, not because he was dreading the interview with the dowager, but because he wanted to calm his thoughts. He also didn't want to be a sweaty mess.

As he approached the town house, he took a deep breath. His thoughts might not be entirely calm, but he was no longer angry with Viola. He understood what she'd been trying to do. And he was deeply grateful.

He was also incredibly surprised.

She'd jumped to his defense with breathtaking speed and a total lack of forethought—both for himself and for her. He knew she thought this wasn't something to get upset about, that she'd weathered scandal before. But this was different. He wasn't the Earl of Ledbury, and she wasn't going to abandon him at the altar.

He was getting married. To Viola.

It wasn't that he was opposed—he just needed time to adjust. This was not how he would have preferred the most important decision of his life to occur.

He walked up to the door, but before he could

knock, it opened and the butler invited him inside. "You are Mr. Barrett, I presume?"

Of course, he'd been expected. "Yes." Jack immediately noticed the impressive art gracing nearly every inch of the entrance hall and refused to be intimidated by the dowager's wealth and status.

"This way." The butler led him to the right into a grand library with bookshelves along every wall, a large table situated near the front window overlooking the square, and a seating arrangement nestled in front of the fireplace. The dowager sat in a wingback chair closest to the hearth, while Viola sat at one end of a settee that faced toward the window. Both women sat ramrod straight, and while the dowager's expression was coolly expectant, Viola's was serene and yet a bit...vacant. He noted, however, that her hands were clasped firmly in her lap.

Jack bowed deeply to the dowager and then to Viola. "Good evening."

"Sit," the dowager said.

Should he take the other chair near the hearth or sit beside Viola? The politician in him said to sit nearer the dowager, but he was drawn to Viola.

He sat next to her on the settee. Close, but not too close.

The dowager speared him with an intent stare. "Viola has explained everything to me, and while I understand you weren't actually together last night, it doesn't matter. The damage to your reputations is done, and the only way to mitigate it, at least partially, is to wed with haste."

Jack was surprised that Viola had explained "everything" and was eager to know what "everything" entailed. He glanced over at her, but her face was still impassive. "I agree."

"Good. You have never struck me as a fool."

Did that mean she'd been aware of him before today? He found that hard to believe. "Thank you." He didn't know what else to say.

"Can you afford to purchase a license?" the dowager asked.

"Yes."

"Good. The banns will take too long. You need to wed as soon as possible. I propose you wed in one week at St. George's."

"Since you're only proposing, does that mean we get to choose?" Viola asked with more than a touch of sarcasm. It was the first inkling he had as to her thoughts... She was not pleased with this turn of events.

"The date, but not whether you will marry." The dowager glowered at her granddaughter. "Do not prattle on again about not needing to wed. That question has been settled, and Mr. Barrett agrees with me."

Viola glanced at him, then looked down at her lap. He could practically hear her mind turning as if it were a machine.

The dowager returned her attention to Jack. "Mr. Barrett, I should like to host a dinner for our families. Let us plan for the twentieth. I will send a formal invitation to your father."

Jack inclined his head. His father... He was going to be astounded. "Thank you, Your Grace."

The dowager surprised him by rising. He jumped to his feet. "I have high expectations, Mr. Barrett, and you will not disappoint me, I am sure. You are a bright young man with a promising future. This will elevate your status, and I am confident you will bring honor and prestige to our family." She looked at Viola then, and her gaze softened the slightest bit. "I also expect you will make my granddaughter happy. She deserves nothing less."

Viola's head snapped up. She gazed at her grandmother with surprise—and love.

The dowager's momentary tenderness evaporated, and she was the regal autocrat once more. "Now then, I shall leave the two of you alone to discuss your future. Do not be too long." She gave Jack a pointed look, but he wasn't at all sure what she was trying to convey.

Then she departed the library, closing the door behind her.

Closing the door. What the hell did that mean in this context? Jack had never quite understood the aristocracy, and now that he was about to marry into that class, he was even less sure about them.

"I'm so sorry, Jack."

He turned to face Viola. She'd only turned her head and now blinked at him, her beautiful blue eyes sad.

He reached into her lap and took her hand. "Why?"

"I never meant to force you into marriage. We don't have to go through with it, regardless of what my grandmother says. I'll move to the country if I must."

"You aren't moving anywhere. Except to my house, I suppose." His bachelor house. It wasn't that it was small. It just wasn't where he'd imagined living with a wife and children. *Children?* What on earth was happening today!

Jack took a deep breath to try to stop the sudden racing of his heart. It matched the world around him, which seemed to be moving at an alarming pace. He'd barely come to grips with the idea of marriage— and truly, he still hadn't—and now he was to wed in a week?

And yet he looked at Viola and thought of all the wonderful things that could mean. For once, he wouldn't have to suffer through days when he didn't see her or wonder when he might encounter her next.

He'd also be able to kiss her whenever he liked. Hell, he could do more than kiss her.

They could discuss books and politics—anything they wanted—at all hours of the day. Spending time with her, he realized, was the thing he liked most.

"We don't need to wed," Viola repeated. "Truly."

"I disagree, and I don't wish to argue about it. I refuse to allow you to suffer the scandal."

Her eyes narrowed, showing him more of the feisty woman he'd come to know. "You refuse to allow me?"

"Viola, I don't *want* you to. How can that be wrong of me?"

"Are you worried about scandal for yourself?" she asked. "Grandmama is right. You have a promising future, and I may have ruined it. Although, I'd still argue that I perhaps saved it by providing you an alibi for last night."

"My alibi came at the cost of a scandal, whether we're worried about it or not." he said wryly. "But no, I'm not overly concerned about my future. I won't lie and say it didn't even occur to me, but I am far more concerned about you."

"And I've told you not to be. I've suffered worse."

He arched a brow at her. "Has anyone ever told you you're stubborn?"

"Only my parents, my grandmother, my brother, my maid on occasion, probably Blenheim—our butler. No, not Blenheim. He would never. But I've seen it in his eyes."

Jack tried not to laugh and failed.

She smiled in return. "I'm glad you aren't angry anymore. I truly am sorry for what happened at the park." Her smile faded, and she angled her body toward him. "Can we assume Caldwell and Sir Humphrey are behind the letter I received?"

Jack had thought about that on the walk over from the park and had come to the same conclusion. "They appear to be somehow involved. But how did they know I was at the Bull and Fox last night? I was careful to look around, both when I arrived and when I left. I didn't see them or anyone else I knew." He paused. "That's not precisely true. I knew some of the men at the meeting. Some of them go to the Wicked Duke, but I don't think they're associated with Caldwell or Sir Humphrey. I've never seen them together, and they would have no reason to seek the other's company."

"Except they're all together at the Wicked Duke. Maybe they went there after the meeting last night and saw Caldwell and Sir Humphrey."

"Who just happened to ask if I was at the meeting?"

She shrugged. "I don't know. I'm trying to puzzle this out. Did you go to the Wicked Duke afterward?"

"No, I went home." It had been a rare occasion, and now he wished he'd gone. "I'll stop in tonight after I visit my father." He needed to tell him in person about the betrothal.

"I'll meet you there."

He should have seen that coming. "Viola, I don't think it's wise for you to continue as Tavistock, especially now that your grandmother knows the secret."

"Why? She didn't tell me to stop."

He exhaled, knowing he was fighting a losing battle. For now. He intended to put an end to Tavistock for her own safety. "I can't meet you there until ten at the earliest, and perhaps even eleven."

"I will arrive around ten, and I'll try to wait for you. Hurry."

She actually didn't have to ask. He was already counting the minutes until he'd see her again.

He stood. "I must go."

She rose next to him. "That's it? My grandmother closes the door and leaves us alone in here, and you're just going to go?"

He grinned at her. "She told us not to be too long. Were you hoping I'd ravish you in the space of a quarter hour?" He was sorely tempted to try.

She sighed. "I was hoping that if I'd gone to the trouble to cause a scandal, I may as well do something scandalous."

"Is that right?" He curled his arm around her waist and pulled her against him.

She gasped in surprise but eagerly twined her arms around his neck. "That is more what I had in mind."

He tipped his head down and kissed her, licking along her lower lip. She pushed up into him, her breasts pressing into his chest as she touched her tongue to his. He lost himself in her embrace until she pulled back he wasn't sure how much later.

Opening his eyes, he saw her incline her head toward the front window. "The sheer draperies provide a modicum of privacy, but it's not absolute."

Disappointment welled inside him, but he needed to go anyway. Besides, the dowager could decide at any moment that they'd been in here long enough.

He kissed her temple, his lips lingering against her sweet-smelling flesh. "I'll see you tonight."

"For perhaps my last outing as Tavistock."

He looked down at her in surprise. "I was afraid I was going to have to work hard to persuade you to stop."

"As I told you before, I'm eager, not stupid. Even I can see when I've pushed to the very edge. I can always create a new identity." Her blue eyes sparkled with mischief.

He narrowed his eyes at her. "I'm not sure I like that. We'll discuss it later." He kissed her again, then forced himself to leave.

As he walked to the end of the square to hail a hack, he wondered how his father would take the news of his marriage. Jack smiled, thinking his father was going to be very happy.

And that made Jack happy.

❧

*B*y ten that night, Viola was ensconced at a table in the main salon at the Wicked Duke. She had yet to see Jack—or Caldwell and Sir Humphrey.

"Eastleigh!"

Val scanned the room and, seeing Viola, came directly to her table. One of the barmaids delivered his tankard of ale before he was even seated. He, of course, knew she would be here because, per their agreement, she'd sent him a note.

He lifted his mug and whispered, "Congratulations."

She scowled at him and didn't lift her beer in return. "Shh."

"No one heard me. Besides, maybe I'm congratulating you on buying a new horse."

Ironically, Viola knew some men found that to be more exciting than getting married. Not that she was getting married. No, there had to be a way out of it, and yet she was concerned that Jack was intent on actually doing it. Especially since he'd apparently gone to see his father tonight.

She'd considered asking him not to, but her efforts to persuade him that the marriage wasn't necessary were not being heard. Was that because he actually wanted to marry her? No, she couldn't believe that. He'd always been clear in his priorities—he was focused on his career and didn't have time for a wife at present.

Unfortunately, she'd taken that choice away from him. Well, she could give it back to him too. She'd left one man at the altar. What was another?

If she could do it. Jack was different from Edmund. Jack understood her. He valued her. He admired her. She wasn't sure she'd ever find another man like him. Furthermore, she wasn't sure she wanted to.

And for that reason, she wasn't sure she could force him into marriage, which was what this felt like. Was it any wonder she didn't want to be congratulated?

"Grandmama is quite thrilled," Val said.

"Thrilled? How on earth could that ever describe our grandmother?"

Val chuckled. "You have a point." He glanced around. "Is Barrett here yet? And what does he think of"—his gaze raked over her—"that?"

He still kept his voice low, but Viola really didn't want to discuss this here. "Can we save this conversation for another time?"

"Yes, yes. I'm just delighted for you, that's all. I sincerely hope you and he will be as happy as Isabelle and I are."

"Colehaven!"

Val glanced toward the door. "Will you excuse me? I need to speak with Cole."

"Absolutely." She was more than happy to be rid of him.

Giles Langford and Hugh Tarleton came in a few minutes later and joined her. She liked both of them and realized she was going to miss being one of the denizens of the Wicked Duke. She would miss the collegiality, the billiards, and the blessed independence of it all.

"Caldwell! Sir Humphrey!"

Viola's ears pricked up, and her pulse sped. She watched as the two men entered, and plotted how she would approach them. Only she never got a chance.

Val and Cole blocked them from coming farther into the pub. A moment later, they'd ushered the pair outside, and when they returned, Cole made an announcement.

"Caldwell and Sir Humphrey are no longer welcome at the Wicked Duke. They insulted our good friend Jack Barrett this afternoon, and generally behaved in a reprehensible manner with regard to Eastleigh's sister. For that reason, we have tossed them out."

"If they insulted Barrett, good!" Giles called.

There was resounding agreement, and Viola couldn't help but feel a burst of pride even while she was annoyed at being deprived of her quarry. She excused herself from the table and managed to sneak away into the private salon and then out through the rear entrance. Hastening her stride, she rushed around to the Haymarket in the hope that she could catch Caldwell and Sir Humphrey.

Luck was on her side as she saw them farther down the street. Thinking it would be best to have a "chance encounter," she saw an opening in the traffic and dashed across the street. Then she ran up the opposite side and crossed back over so she could run into them.

She fought to catch her breath before she spoke. "Caldwell, Sir Humphrey, pleasant evening to you both."

"It is not," Sir Humphrey complained.

"I'm sorry to hear that," she said. "I'm just headed to the Wicked Duke. Why don't you join me for an ale, unless you've just come from there?" She acted as though she hadn't witnessed their expulsion.

"We *have* just come from there. For the last time," Caldwell said with considerable acid. "I might recommend you stay away. Eastleigh and Colehaven have gone mad and sided with that radical, Barrett."

The perfect segue to see what they would tell her… "I heard about what happened in the park today. Was he really at that Spencean meeting?"

Caldwell nodded firmly. "Without question."

"And yet it *has* been questioned," Viola prodded.

Sir Humphrey curled his lip. "By that stupid chit —Eastleigh's sister."

Viola bit her tongue lest she show them how she wasn't remotely stupid. Instead, she went along with them to encourage their continued sharing of information. "You think she was lying for him?"

"Of course she was. Barrett is a known radical sympathizer, as are several other members of Parliament. He was undoubtedly at that meeting last night."

"You sound awfully confident," Viola said, desperate to know how they could be.

Sir Humphrey leaned forward and, looking quite smug, lowered his voice. "Because we have a man on the inside."

Viola froze. *That* was the story. "What do you mean?"

"Nothing," Caldwell snapped. "Sir Humphrey has had too much to drink tonight. I need to see him home. Evening, Tavistock." Caldwell grabbed Sir Humphrey's elbow and dragged him along the pavement.

Viola turned and watched them walk away, Caldwell furiously talking into Sir Humphrey's ear. Clearly, he'd spoken out of turn.

Oh, she couldn't wait to tell Jack what she'd learned!

Pivoting, she practically skipped back to the Wicked Duke. And then, because luck was really with her that evening, she ran into Jack just as he arrived outside the tavern.

He grinned at her. "Excellent timing."

"No, no. I've already been inside, and Caldwell and Sir Humphrey have been banned." She grabbed Jack's elbow much the same as Caldwell had grabbed Sir Humphrey and started down the Haymarket.

Jack moved alongside her, and she dropped her hand. "What happened?"

"Caldwell and Sir Humphrey came in, and my brother and Cole expelled them. Forever. They told everyone he'd insulted you—and me, Viola me, not Tavistock—and were no longer welcome at the Wicked Duke."

"That's...very nice."

"It was bloody brilliant!" She laughed. "You should have heard everyone. You are clearly far more liked than either of them."

"That is unsurprising," he murmured before leading her across the street to Charles Street.

"Where are we going?" she asked.

He stopped on the other side of the street. "I don't know. I was simply walking the way I usually do when I leave the Wicked Duke—to my house."

"Oh." She suddenly wanted to go to his house. "Can I see it? I can tell you what I learned along the way. Then I can take a hack home."

"Not alone, you won't."

"Fine. Anyway, I'm simply bursting with what I must tell you, so please stop interrupting."

He laughed softly as they made their way into St. James's Square. "I am hardly interrupting. You are not talking fast enough."

She glared at him briefly before launching into her tale. "After Val and Cole threw Caldwell and Sir Humphrey out, I went out the back and went around to the Haymarket where I intercepted them."

"Did you?" He shook his head. "Of course you did. You know no fear, Viola. And you *should*."

She exhaled in exasperation. "Can I please finish?"

"Please," he said amiably.

"And don't interrupt again, because you really are taking the fun out of it, and this is such a good story!"

"I am positively aquiver with anticipation."

"Stop that. I queried them about how they knew you were at the meeting. And before you say that was dangerous, they are the ones who brought it up." That wasn't precisely what happened, but they'd certainly given her an opportunity to ask. "They were absolutely confident you were at the meeting last night, and when I pressed them about it, Sir Humphrey's loose tongue got the better of him. He said they knew it for certain because they had an *informer*."

They'd crossed the square and were now at the juncture of King Street. Jack stopped and turned to stare at her. "He said what?"

She nodded vigorously. "*That's* the story, Jack. What do you think it means? What sort of man?"

He rubbed his hand along his cheek and jaw. "I don't know. I'm trying to recall who was there last night, but I can't think of anyone who stood out. But then if they'd embedded someone in the Spencean Philanthropists, I would guess they wouldn't be conspicuous."

"It's not as if they'd wear a sign that reads 'spy.'"

Jack gave her a wry look, his mouth twisting into a half smile. "No, they would not." He was silent a moment, and she wondered what he was thinking. "This is going to take some pondering as to our next move. I think it may be time for me to solicit additional help from my colleagues. This seems to be a far bigger situation than I'd imagined."

He gestured to the house on the corner. "This is where I live."

Viola pivoted and took in the smart town house. It wasn't large, but it was neat, and the green door and bow window at the front were most inviting.

"I'll hail a hack," he said, turning back toward the street.

She clasped his elbow again, and he stopped. "Can I see the inside?"

He hesitated before saying, "I suppose you could."

"You can't say it's a scandal, because I already did that. And since I did earn it and didn't get to do anything truly scandalous in the library earlier, I think you owe me a night of scandal."

His dark brows arched high on his forehead. "*I* owe *you?*"

She stepped closer. "Maybe we owe each other."

He swore under his breath, then started to take her hand. Letting her go, he swore again. "I will be very glad when you are no longer disguised as a man."

Viola couldn't help but giggle as he led her up the steps to his door. He opened it and held it while she moved into the small but elegant entrance hall. Pale gray marble gleamed beneath her feet. To the left, she saw his study—the room with the bow window that faced the street. Stairs marched up the right wall, while a corridor extended back from the entrance hall.

A middle-aged butler came into the hall.

"Good evening, Gardner," Jack said. "Allow me to present my betrothed, Lady Viola Fairfax. Viola, this is my butler."

Viola gaped at him before turning her attention to

the butler. "Pleased to meet you, Gardner. Pardon my…costume. I was at a masquerade." No one would ever believe she'd gone to a masquerade dressed so thoroughly as a man, but Gardner was evidently a butler of exceeding grace and talent, and his gaze didn't reflect even a hint of surprise or affront.

He bowed to her. "It is my pleasure, my lady. We are most delighted to hear of your upcoming marriage. On behalf of the staff, we are eager to serve you."

"Thank you, Gardner. Mr. Barrett is just going to give me a tour." She hoped he was, anyway. Actually, she hoped he was going to do far more.

"Exactly so," Jack said smoothly. He gestured toward the back of the house. "That way is the dining room as well as a small morning room that opens to my miniscule garden. Let us go upstairs."

She smiled at the butler before preceding Jack up the stairs. On the first floor, he gestured toward the front of the house to a wide doorway. "The drawing room, not that I entertain much." He turned and pointed to the rear of the house. "A bedroom for guests. Not that anyone comes to visit." He took her hand again, and this time, he didn't let go.

Guiding her up to the second floor, he took her to the front of the house and opened the door to a small sitting room. Leading her through it, they emerged in a bedchamber. His bedchamber.

He let go of her hand and walked farther into the room until he stood in the center. "And this is where I sleep. When I am not tortured by thoughts of you."

Viola took off her hat and tossed it aside, then did the same with her gloves. "You're tortured by thoughts of me?" She sauntered toward him and began to pluck the pins that held her wig in place.

"Positively bedeviled." He removed his coat and set it on a chair near the window that surely overlooked the street below. She couldn't tell because the dark green draperies were closed against the night. A small fire burned in the hearth, and lanterns glowed from either side of the bed. Overall, it was dim, but there was enough light for her to see him.

When all the pins were free, she dislodged the wig and set it atop a table with the pins. Then she peeled the whiskers from her face. "Would it surprise you to know I have been tortured similarly? When I close my eyes, I feel your lips on mine. When I lie in bed, I imagine you beside me. On top of me. *Inside* me."

"Viola, dear God." He was suddenly before her, his fingers deftly pulling the pins from her upswept hair and tossing them to the floor.

"The pins," she said.

"Can go to the devil." When her hair was free, he plunged his hands into the strands and cupped her head. He stared at her as if he couldn't get enough of looking at her face, then he brought his thumbs down her cheeks to her jaw and over her lips until they met. "You are the most beautiful woman I have ever seen. I don't think I can bear to see you as Tavistock again."

She stuck her tongue out and licked the pads of his thumbs. He groaned and moved his hands to the sides of her head. Then he kissed her, his mouth meeting hers with a towering passion she knew would consume them both. And she could hardly wait.

CHAPTER 13

*J*ack was so glad to see the wig and the whiskers gone. He'd longed to rake his hands through the silken honey of her hair, and it felt better than he'd ever imagined. Now he wanted Tavistock banished for good.

He dragged his mouth from hers and kissed along her jaw as he loosened her cravat. He tugged the silk free and dropped it to the floor. Trailing his lips down her neck, he pulled the collar of her shirt so he could access her collarbone. It wasn't enough.

Passion rising, he pushed at her coat, and together, they cast it aside. He didn't wait for it to fall before he began unbuttoning her waistcoat. A moment later, the garment joined the coat wherever it had landed.

She pulled the shirt from the waistband of her breeches and drew it over her head. But of course she wasn't bare—her breasts were bound, which he'd known they had to be. When he'd kissed and held her in the closet at the ball, her breasts had pressed against his chest in a way they never had when she was dressed as Tavistock.

He longed to unbind her, but first, he wanted her boots off. Guiding her toward the bed, he sat her on the cushioned bench at the end. Then he knelt on the floor and pulled her boots from her feet.

"You are an excellent valet," she said. Her voice had deepened, but not in the way it did when she played Tavistock. This was a sultry, feminine sound that curled deep in his belly.

"We'll see about that when you have to get dressed again." He went to work on her stockings next, and when her feet were bare, he massaged them briefly before pressing his lips to the inside of her calf.

She twitched, then shivered as he kissed his way up to where her breeches started. He lifted his head and knelt between her legs. Looking up into her face, he brushed her hair back and cupped her nape, drawing her down so he could kiss her again.

She put her hands on his shoulders and returned the kiss with a rapture that matched his own. He gripped her hips as she assumed the role of valet, stripping him of his cravat and unbuttoning his waistcoat. Impatient, he helped her, nearly ripping the garment in his haste to tear it off.

She broke the kiss and slid from the bench. "Your turn." She guided him to take her place, then she went about removing his boots.

Her eyes met his and never broke contact the entire time she divested him of his footwear and stockings. It was the most erotic undressing he'd ever experienced. His cock raged with want, and he was nearly panting with desire.

She frowned up at him. "You're still wearing a shirt."

"And you're still wearing breeches."

"So are you," she countered. "Shirt. Off."

He pulled the cotton from his breeches and whisked the garment over his head. "Better?"

Her gaze locked on his bare chest, and her lips parted. "Oh, yes."

"Viola, if you continue to look at me as if I'm a sweetmeat on a tray, I'm going to throw you on the bed and shag you senseless."

She continued to stare at him. "All right." Then she licked her lower lip.

Groaning, Jack clasped her by the biceps and stood. "Enough."

"Not nearly," she murmured before his mouth claimed hers.

He completely gave in to his lust, his lips and tongue devouring her more thoroughly and desperately than any sweetmeat. She was an equal partner in this madness, her hands exploring his shoulders, his back, his hips, then coming up between them. She splayed her palms over his chest, her fingers finding his nipples and rubbing back and forth across the points until he moaned.

It was past time to remove the binding.

He pulled his mouth from hers and led her to the side of the bed so they'd be next to one of the lanterns. "I want to see every inch of you," he whispered, grasping the end of the binding fabric tucked between her breasts.

She lifted her arms so he could easily unwind the muslin. Four times it went around, and with each revelation, his breath caught anew. At last, her breasts bobbed free, and he dropped the fabric, now forgotten, to the floor.

She was absolutely exquisite. He stroked her neck, caressing where it met her collarbone, which swept out in an elegant line to her shoulder. From there, he skimmed his fingertips down to the tempting swell of her breast. With both hands, he cupped her, the weight filling his grasp. He traced his thumbs over the nipples, and they responded instantly, becoming deliciously erect.

He leaned down and drew one into his mouth.

She gasped as her hands clasped the back of his head. With lips and tongue, he tormented her—or tormented himself, depending on one's perspective. But it was the sweetest torture he could imagine. Teasing her and touching her only increased his arousal to an incredible height.

"Jack, please."

He pulled on one nipple with his fingers while he suckled the other. "Please what?" he managed while he moved his mouth to her other breast.

"I don't know exactly." When he pulled hard on her nipple, his lips drawing on her flesh, she cried out. "*Yes.*"

He reached down for the fall of her breeches. Finding the buttons, he worked to set them free. A moment later, he pushed the garment down her hips. He took a tiny step back so he could look at her nude.

He'd imagined her a thousand times like this, but the picture in his mind couldn't compare with the reality. Her hips flared gently from her waist, and golden hair cloaked her sex. He wanted to taste her, but maybe not tonight. He assumed this was her first sexual encounter; however, maybe it wasn't. She'd been betrothed before.

He raised his gaze to her face. "Sorry, I can't seem to stop staring at you. You're so beautiful."

"It's all right. I keep doing the same to you. Except you're *still* wearing breeches."

The frustration in her voice made him chuckle. But then he sobered. "Is this your first time?"

She nodded. "I mean, I kissed Edmund, and he touched me a—"

"Stop, please. I don't want to hear what you and Ledbury did."

"I'd rather talk about what you want to do to me. Can you touch me now? Please?"

She wanted to talk about it? Oh, he could talk

about a hundred things he'd like to do to her. "Where would you like me to touch you?"

"Anywhere. Everywhere."

He touched her breast, stroking along the underside and then lightly pinching the nipple. "Here?"

She gasped and nodded, her lids drooping.

He skimmed his hand down over her rib cage and along her belly, then over to her hip. He caressed the curve there and traveled to her backside, cupping and squeezing her flesh. "Here?"

She put her hands on her shoulders, perhaps to steady herself. He could feel her quivering. "Yes."

Trailing his fingertips back over and around her thigh, he moved them up between her legs until he felt the heat of her. "Here?"

Her hands squeezed his shoulders. "Yes. Please."

She was already wet when he grazed his fingers along her folds. She cried out again, her fingertips digging into his flesh. He found her clitoris then and rubbed against her until she moaned. Then he remembered what she'd said earlier, that she'd wanted him inside her.

He'd kept a tight rein on his control, but it was beginning to slip. Desire and need built to a crescendo within him, and he stroked a finger inside her. She moaned again, more loudly this time, and he kissed her in a wild frenzy.

He wanted to hear her scream. He wanted to *make* her scream.

Jack lifted her onto the bed and quickly tore his breeches away. Climbing up, he knelt between her legs and kissed her belly. Then he pressed on her inner thighs and put his mouth on her sex.

"Jack!"

He lifted his head, not to look up at her, but to ask, "Yes?"

"What are you doing?"

He licked along her sex and used his thumb and fingers to tease her clitoris. "Making you scream, I hope."

"I *can't* scream. Your staff will think something is wrong."

"My staff will think I'm pleasuring the woman who will soon be my wife. Which is precisely what I'm doing." He put his tongue inside her and pressed on her clitoris, agitating her flesh until she bucked off the bed and indeed let out a wail.

He felt her orgasm coming, her muscles tensing as he put his finger back inside her and stroked in and out. It was barely a moment before she cried out once more and her flesh shuddered around him.

Rising onto his knees, he looked down at her satisfaction-glazed expression with a truly absurd amount of male pride.

She opened her eyes and tried to focus on him. "I never expected *that.*"

"Good. I shall endeavor to always surprise you."

A shadow of unease crept over her features. "That's not all, is it?"

"It is if you want it to be." He prayed she didn't want it to be.

She looked up at him with a thoroughly petulant and provocative expression that made his cock harden even more. "You promised to shag me senseless, and I'm not leaving until you do."

~

*T*he need she'd felt a few minutes before, which she'd thought he'd satisfied, came roaring back. She couldn't stop staring at the gorgeous expanse of his muscled chest and the alluring dip between his waist, hip, and groin. Jack, she decided, had to be the perfect male specimen, far more attractive than any painting or sculpture she'd seen.

And then there was his manhood. His *cock*. That was the word she'd giggled over several years ago when discussing the act of sexual intercourse with her friends. It had seemed a silly word, but now, looking at the hard shaft, it seemed somehow appropriate.

She leaned up and reached for him, grazing her fingertips across the moist head peeking forth from his foreskin.

He sucked in a breath.

"Is this all right?"

"It's marvelous. Stupendous. The single greatest moment of my life." Except he sounded as if he were in pain.

"I'm not sure I believe you." She wrapped her hand around him, loving how warm and velvety he felt. "You sound as if I'm torturing you."

"And so you are." Now, he sounded as if he couldn't breathe.

"Am I? Here I was trying to give you pleasure." She pulled her hand away. "Perhaps I should stop."

His hand closed over hers, and he brought it back to his cock, curling her fingers around the base. "Start here and glide up." He showed her what he wanted. "Slow, fast, whatever you want to do."

"I want to put you in my mouth."

"Oh God. Not tonight, Viola. Next time."

"Why not? That's what you did."

"Because I don't want your first time to be me spilling my seed down your throat. Though at the rate we're going, I'm going to be spilling my seed all over your thighs. Just—" He put his hand over hers and guided himself to her sex.

"Are we doing this now?" she asked.

He looked into her eyes. "Unless you've changed your mind."

"No, please shag me." She parted her legs farther and urged him to move inside her. "Senseless, if you don't mind."

"I don't think I'll be able to do anything else." He pressed into her, moving slowly, his shaft sliding within her sheath as if they'd done this a thousand times. It felt so natural, so right, as if they'd been made exclusively for each other.

She felt a twinge of discomfort as she stretched to accommodate him. He stopped, looking down at her as he smoothed her hair back from her forehead. "All right?" he asked her tenderly.

She nodded. "Don't stop." Through the slight ache, she glimpsed the pleasure.

He continued forward until she felt quite full. "I'm just going to sit here for a moment." The discomfort began to fade, and she wanted to move.

"Actually, I think I'd rather you get out."

He immediately started to withdraw. "I'm sorry."

"And then come back in. Isn't that what we're supposed to do? The shagging, I mean." She groaned in frustration. "I don't think I can communicate worth a fig right now."

He laughed softly, then kissed her. "You are communicating just fine." He eased back in, then withdrew again slowly, then thrust just as slowly.

"This is quite nice. But I think I want more than nice. Faster, if you please."

"Are you sure you're ready? I'm not hurting you?"

She shook her head, and he pressed forward, hitting a spot he hadn't before, and need crashed over her. She clasped his hips and squeezed. "*Move.*"

He kissed her again, his mouth open and wet, his tongue driving into her as his cock did the same. He moved hard and fast, and she arched up to meet him, their bodies moving in perfect rhythm. The climax she'd experienced before began to build anew, and she splayed her hands across his lower back as he guided her legs to curl around his hips.

Oh, this was even better. He drove more deeply still, and she crested the top of the mountain, diving into a rapturous abyss that knew no end.

He thrust a few more times, then she heard him cry out her name. He continued to move with a less frenzied pace, and soon he ceased entirely. His body came down on top of her, and the warm weight of him was delicious. She wrapped her arms around him and kissed his cheek, his mouth, his neck, nuzzling him.

After some time, he rolled to the side and drew her against him. "Should we clean up?" she whispered.

"Not yet. I just want to hold you. Then I'll take you home."

Viola sighed as she snuggled against him. How could he take her home when she felt like she was already there?

CHAPTER 14

"What on earth are you writing?" Grandmama asked from her chair near the fireplace.

Viola looked up from the table where she'd been pouring out ideas about a book. She wasn't sure how long she'd been scratching the pen across the parchment. "I'm...writing." Grandmama would tell her writing a novel was a waste of time, especially now that she was getting married.

She was getting married.

Last night had been transformative. She'd truly felt she'd been home in Jack's arms. The thought of not marrying him made the air leave her lungs and a hole open up in the vicinity of her heart.

Because she loved him. Now she knew—and was ready to admit it—and in hindsight, she felt like a fool. She'd been falling in love with him for a fortnight now, and she could only hope he'd been doing the same with her. She'd almost told him last night, but what if he didn't love her in return? He clearly cared for her and he was going to marry her, but was it the same as this overwhelming...passion she had for him? Every moment away from him was like an eternity, and every moment with him was joy.

"Is it a love letter?" Grandmama asked.

Viola snapped her gaze to her grandmother and caught the end of a rare, faint smile. "No, it is not a love letter."

"I assumed it was. Your lovesickness is clear. I am glad the wedding is happening soon." She stood from her chair. "Time for my nap."

She passed Blenheim, who inclined his head as she left the library. The butler brought a letter to Viola. "This arrived for you from His Grace, my lady."

She smiled up at him. "Thank you, Blenheim."

Tearing open the missive, Viola saw there was a second letter tucked inside. She read the first one, from Val, which said the other had arrived at the Wicked Duke for Tavistock. Viola's pulse twitched and her heart began to pound as she opened the second letter.

Dear Tavistock,

Come to The Black Hare on Villers Street at three o'clock if you want to lern the identity of the informer within the Spenseans.

She frowned at the paper. The handwriting was unfamiliar—it was not the same as the previous letter addressed to Tavistock. This one was rather sloppy with ink splotches and contained spelling errors. She assumed he meant Villiers Street.

She glanced at the clock on the mantel. It was scarcely two. If she hurried, she could make it. And yet, she shouldn't go alone. Perhaps Jack could meet her. She'd send a note to him at Westminster asking him to meet her at The Black Hare.

What if he didn't receive the note in time? Or what if he couldn't get away? She'd go, and if he didn't arrive, she'd leave. There could be no harm in that.

Grabbing a new piece of parchment, she dashed off the note, then stood and went into the entrance hall. "Blenheim, this must be delivered to Westminster immediately. To Mr. Jack Barrett."

He took the missive with a nod. "I'll dispatch a footman at once."

"Thank you." She smiled, then hurried upstairs to don her Tavistock costume. And she'd thought last night had been the last occasion she'd do so.

For the first time, she dreaded the prospect of binding her breasts, flattening her hair so the wig would fit, and gluing the whiskers to her cheeks. Hopefully, *this* would be the last time.

It was nearly three when the hired hack arrived on Villiers Street just down from The Black Hare. Viola asked the driver to stay for a few minutes and gave him extra coin to do so. He agreed, but said he wouldn't wait all day.

She scanned the pavement and the other side of the street for Jack but didn't see him. Pacing, she watched for another hack. Perhaps he'd gone into The Black Hare.

Walking toward the tavern, she hesitated outside the door. She shouldn't go in, not without him. Instead, she tried to peer in the window, but it was dingy and she couldn't identify any of the people inside.

Frustrated and disappointed because it looked like she wasn't going to learn the identity of the informer, she turned and started back toward her hack. Suddenly, strong arms grabbed her and pulled her into the narrow alley beside the pub. But that was all she saw, for a sack came down over her head, plunging her into darkness.

She started to yell—no, it was a scream, a feminine scream, and she didn't care. A hand came over her mouth, silencing her.

"Christ, Tavistock sounds like a woman!" Her captor tightened his grip. "Keep quiet, or we'll have to shoot you."

"We will?" This was a new voice. There were two of them.

"Yes!" the first one hissed.

While they argued, they dragged her, presumably through the alley. They each held one of her arms, and one of them kept his hand over her mouth. She heard a door open, and they pushed her roughly inside. Then they hauled her up a flight of stairs, but it was too awkward for the one man to keep his hand on her mouth. She started to scream again, and the man above her on the stairs hit her. She stumbled back, but the man below her caught her.

"Bloody hell!" the man holding her cried.

"Keep him—or her—quiet, or I will shoot him. Or her."

Viola felt something poking into her stomach. It didn't necessarily feel like a pistol, but how could she know? She couldn't see a thing, and it wasn't as if she'd ever had a gun shoved into her gut before.

"Tie something over his mouth," the man above her said.

A moment later, fingers felt over the sack covering her face. When he found her mouth, she considered trying to bite him, but didn't think she'd do much damage through the cloth. Furthermore, there was probably a pistol trained on her midsection.

The man behind her tied something around her mouth, forcing the sack between her lips. She tasted dust and grime, and nausea swirled in her belly.

They pulled her up the rest of the stairs and into a room. She heard the door close, and then she was thrown into a chair. One of the men pulled her arms behind her and tied her wrists together.

Viola, whose heart was already threatening to

beat clear out of her chest, tensed. She wanted to ask what they wanted, but she couldn't talk. When she tried, all that came out were muffled sounds.

Fingers slid beneath the gag tied around her face as they separated it from the sack, which they then pushed up past her nose, but left covering her eyes. She shuddered from revulsion at having the man touch her so intimately. Then he pulled at her whiskers, peeling them away from her skin.

"The sideburns are fake," the man said.

"Bloody hell, he is a woman," the man with the pistol swore. Both of them sounded somewhat familiar, but Viola couldn't quite place them.

"Now what do we do?" the first man asked.

"Depends on who she is," pistol-man responded.

Viola tried to yell that she was the Duke of Eastleigh's sister.

"Can't tell without revealing her face, and then she'll be able to see us."

"And we can't have that." The man shoved the pistol in her side, making her gasp. "Tavistock, you've caused far more trouble than you're worth. Now we have to decide what to do about it."

Fear curled in Viola's gut, and she feared she was going to be sick. She never should have come today. She'd thought her plan was sound, and she'd been about to return to the hack since Jack wasn't here.

Jack.

She could only pray he would arrive before… She wasn't sure what, and she was afraid to find out.

～

*N*ear the end of his second long meeting of the afternoon, Jack received a note. He would have set it aside, but he recognized Viola's handwriting. Smiling to himself, as he'd been doing all day because he couldn't stop thinking of the night before, he opened it. The smile turned to a frown by the time he finished.

Standing, he apologized to his colleagues and left in haste. He caught a hack and told the driver to hurry to Villiers Street. He arrived outside The Black Hare and looked around for Viola—rather, Tavistock.

Not seeing her, he went inside the tavern and asked if anyone had seen the young man. When no one had, his concern flared into full alarm. Dashing back outside, he scanned both sides of the street more closely. This time, he caught sight of a hack positioned just a short way down the street.

He ran to the hack and called up to the driver, "I don't suppose you've seen a young man? Shorter than average, rather skinny." Skinny didn't remotely describe Viola's curves, but for a man, she was slight at best.

The driver's brow furrowed beneath his hat. "I have. He paid me to wait for a few minutes. I was about to leave, and then I saw a couple of gents drag him into that alley."

Jack gaped at him. "And you just sat there and watched?"

"I don't want any trouble," the driver said. "I've been sitting here the past few minutes trying to decide what to do. I'm just one man, and not even a full one." He knocked on his boot, and the hollow sound told Jack he had a wooden leg.

Swearing, Jack pointed toward the alley next to the tavern. "They took him through there?"

The driver nodded. "Maybe ten minutes ago."

"Two men, you say?" Jack confirmed.

At the driver's nod, Jack strode back to the tavern, passing the alley and ignoring the sharp pain of distress in his chest and gut. It wouldn't do to go storming into the alley and try to find them. He hoped they were somewhere in the tavern.

Inside, he approached the barkeep. "Do you have a back room where a couple of gentlemen might be? I have a meeting." He slid a bank note across the bar to the man.

"There's a room upstairs. Couple of fellows are using it today. Go on through the back there. Door on the right leads to the stairs."

"Thank you." Jack barely finished uttering the words before he was through the back door. It might not be them, but it was all he had right now.

Pushing the door open, he moved cautiously into a short corridor. There was a second door to his right and based on its location, he guessed it led to the alley. Hope bloomed in his chest, and he crept up the stairs, careful to make as little noise as possible.

He paused halfway up, worried that he didn't have a weapon. What if they were armed? But he couldn't leave, not if she was up there now and in grave danger. Maybe there was something he could use downstairs.

He hurried back down and went back through the doorway. He found a small storage closet. Inside was a variety of cleaning implements, including a broom. It wasn't much, but it was better than nothing, and he'd taken his fair share of fencing lessons.

Inspiration struck, and he broke the handle over his knee. This left him with a jagged-ended pole. Perfect. Not really, but it would have to do.

Retracing his steps, Jack went up the stairs to a narrow landing. A single sconce burning on the stairs didn't provide much illumination. There were three doors. Jack bent his head to each, listening. At the second one, he heard voices. Then he heard the definitive sound of a muffled shriek.

He threw the door open and rushed inside,

wielding the jagged pole. A shocked pair of gentlemen stared at him. Pennington and Sir Humphrey. They stood on either side of Viola, and Pennington had his fingers jabbed into Viola's side.

She tried to squirm away from him, but her arms were tied behind her back, and her mobility was limited.

Rage swam in Jack's vision. "What the hell are you doing?"

Viola yelled something that might have been "Jack," but he couldn't say for sure because they had a gag around her mouth. Oh, he was going to commit violence. He just had to decide who would receive his wrath first.

Sir Humphrey's eyes rounded. "Barrett! What are you doing here?"

"That hardly matters. Back away from her." He realized he hadn't used the right pronoun, but he didn't care. Keeping Viola safe was the only thing that mattered. "Pennington, what are you doing poking her like that? Take the sack off her head. *Now.*" Jack moved forward and waved the broken broom handle in the man's face.

Pennington let out a sound of fear and hurried to remove the sack. Viola's hat sailed away with it, and her wig shifted.

Sir Humphrey gasped. "Eastleigh's sister!"

Apparently, they hadn't realized Tavistock was a woman. Wait, they'd had to. Her whiskers were in her lap. It seemed they hadn't known her identity.

Viola's eyes found his, and she sagged in relief. Jack, meanwhile, was ready to commit murder.

"Take off the gag," Jack growled. "I can't believe I have to ask." He thrust the broom handle next to Pennington's cheek.

He yelped, then quickly removed Viola's gag.

Jack waved the pole toward Sir Humphrey. "Untie her!"

When she was free, she jumped up from the chair and dashed to Jack's side. He put his arm around her and held her close. She buried her face in his neck. "I'm so sorry," she whispered. "When I didn't see you, I tried to leave, but they grabbed me."

"Shh." He kissed her temple. "I've got you now."

He glared at Pennington and Sir Humphrey. "Explain yourselves before Bow Street arrives."

They both paled. "We only meant to frighten him," Sir Humphrey said, his voice high with desperation. "Her. Tavistock."

"We didn't know he was a woman," Pennington said.

Viola glared at them. "You didn't even have a gun, did you?"

Pennington shook his head. "We just wanted to frighten you. Sir Humphrey said something foolish to you last night, and Caldwell said he had to fix it." He glowered at Sir Humphrey. "He convinced me to help him, as he and Caldwell have been doing all along."

Caldwell. Jack hadn't really thought that he—and these men—would resort to such measures to eliminate him, a political foe. "Where is Caldwell?"

Sir Humphrey wrung his hands. "He told us to take care of it. It was my mistake to mention the informer. No one was supposed to know. *I* wasn't even supposed to know."

"And you told a reporter," Viola said with disgust.

"What was your objective—along with Caldwell? You accused me of meeting with the Spenceans, and you're trying to link me to the attack on the Prince Regent. Why?" Jack demanded.

"We just wanted you out of the way," Sir Humphrey said. "You're a thorn in our sides, always prattling on about reform. You'd see our boroughs redrawn, and then we wouldn't have seats."

"You don't deserve seats," Viola spat. "And that was before you became criminals."

"Caldwell wanted to ruin your reputation—to get you expelled from the Commons," Pennington whined. "Blame him."

"You are not blameless," Jack said darkly. He handed the broom handle to Viola. "Hold this."

Crossing the space between himself and Pennington, he planted the man a facer, sending him reeling backward. Then he turned and did the same to Sir Humphrey, knocking that man to the floor.

"You're lucky if that's all I do to you." Jack went back to Viola and wrapped her in his arms. He kissed her, then took the broom handle back before addressing the men once more. "Stay here until Bow Street arrives. If you don't, they know where you live. And if you tell a soul who Tavistock really is, I'll hunt you down and make what's left of your miserable lives positively abhorrent. Do you understand me?"

They both nodded vigorously, Pennington cowering near the corner and Sir Humphrey huddled on the floor.

Turning, he took Viola's hand and led her from the room, closing the door firmly behind him. He hurried down the stairs and decided they'd best leave through the back door into the alley.

Once they were outside, he felt her body start to wilt. He dropped the broom handle and turned, taking her into his arms and holding her tightly against his chest. "You're safe now."

"I was afraid you wouldn't find me. And just when everything had seemed so perfect." She pulled back and looked up into his face, her wig askew, but her face was all Viola and so beloved.

"Of course I would find you. I would search to the

corners of the earth, to the very end of time. You are mine, Viola. I love you."

Tears of joy slipped down her cheeks, and he wiped the moisture away. "Don't cry, sweetheart."

"I can't help it. I've never been this happy. I love you too."

He kissed her, and they clasped each other as if the world might tear them apart. It was a few moments before she took a shuddering breath and looked up into his face once more. "I hadn't planned to marry you."

He cocked his head to the side as a sliver of ice shot down his spine. "What do you mean?"

"I tried to tell you we didn't have to wed. You didn't want to get married."

"I do now. Scandal or not, I want you, Viola. I love you. I *need* you." He stroked her cheek. "You wouldn't have left me at the altar, would you?"

She shook her head. "No. I couldn't have done it. I tried so hard not to love you, not to be vulnerable—I wasn't sure you loved me in return."

He laughed. "How could you not know? I was fairly certain my heart was on my sleeve for all to see."

She smiled up at him, her hands moving across his back. "I can see it now. And it's mine."

"It is indeed." He kissed her once more, then took her hand and led her from the alley. "Come, we need to get you home, and I need to visit Bow Street."

"I'm coming with you. For the book."

He paused when they reached the street and looked at her. "The book? You mean the article you're writing."

She shook her head. "I think I'd rather write a book. Unless we can find out who the informer is and why he infiltrated the Spenceans."

"That's what I want to do." The idea that Caldwell

or other members of Parliament had planted someone inside the Spenceans was incredibly troubling. What had been their motive? Was it to implicate Jack all along, or was it bigger than that? He wanted to address Caldwell, and he would.

He hailed a hack, and they were soon on their way to Berkeley Square.

CHAPTER 15

*M*ore than an hour later, Viola sat in an office at Bow Street while Jack paced in front of the hearth. The weather had turned dreary, and there was a chill in the air, but even the warm fire couldn't banish the feeling of foreboding.

"Why is this taking so long?" Jack asked.

They'd arrived some time ago after stopping in Berkeley Square so Viola could quickly transform herself from Tavistock to Lady Viola. Then they'd hurried here in Grandmama's coach, which was now parked outside.

Thankfully, Grandmama had still been napping, because it would have taken far too long to explain what they were about. And why it was necessary for them to go to Bow Street. Together. Alone.

It was a good thing they'd already caused a scandal and were on their way to the altar.

The door opened, and Viola couldn't quite believe who entered. Lord Orford greeted them with a firm nod.

"Good afternoon, Lady Viola." He bowed to her, then turned to Jack, offering his hand. "Barrett."

Jack gripped the man's hand, but his expression

was a mix of curiosity and skepticism. "I thought we were going to see a runner."

"Not for this." Orford sat down in a chair angled next to the short settee where Viola sat. "Would you mind taking a seat?" He looked at Jack and gestured next to Viola.

Frowning, Jack descended to the settee. She could feel the tension swirling in him.

"Why are you here?" Jack asked.

"It's complicated. The clerk, Mr. Stafford, has asked that I speak with you. I apologize that it took so long for me to arrive."

Jack studied him. "You were still at Westminster?"

"I was. I had to deal with a matter there regarding Mr. Caldwell."

"He is part of the crime," Jack said with disgust.

"I've been apprised of what happened with Lady Viola." He looked toward Viola, and his gaze softened with sympathy. "I'm terribly sorry for the trauma they caused you."

Jack sat forward, his mouth hard and his gaze sparking with fury. "Out with it, Orford. Why are you here, and what have you to do with informers and instigators and rumors of my involvement with the attack on the Prince Regent?"

"I shall try to explain as best I can, but there are aspects of this…situation that are extremely sensitive and cannot be disclosed."

The foreboding Viola had felt intensified.

Orford looked to Jack. "You met Mr. Castle at the Spencean meeting?" When Jack nodded, he continued. "He is an informer, and I'm afraid he shared your presence at the meeting with Caldwell, whom I'd hoped would be an aid in this…situation. I unfortunately miscalculated Caldwell's trustworthiness, as well as his honor." He looked at both of them in apology.

Jack gaped at him. "The government has placed an informer in the Spencean Philanthropists—that's madness."

It was as if Orford hadn't even heard him. "I'm sorry this happened. Caldwell had his own objectives that I was not privy to. He'd been looking for a way to get you expelled from your seat and sought to make it look as if you were somehow involved in the attack on the Prince." He shook his head grimly. "Caldwell will no longer be occupying his seat, nor will Pennington or Sir Humphrey. They will not bother you in any way ever again."

Jack narrowed his eyes at Orford. "Do you work for the Home Office?"

Orford didn't respond, and his expression remained bland. To Viola, that seemed as much an admission as if he'd said yes. Especially given the conversations she'd had with him—as if he'd been trying to learn information about the rumor surrounding the attack. Perhaps he'd been doing so on behalf of the Home Office. She reached for Jack's hand and found he was still tense.

He frowned at Orford. "I'm not sure I trust you— or whoever is in charge—to ensure that happens. If anyone threatens or harms my wife, I will not sit idly by."

While she wasn't yet his wife, the word thrilled her. She squeezed his hand and was grateful when he clasped hers in return.

"I fully understand your position. I would feel the same way." Orford glanced toward Viola, and she thought she detected a hint of remorse. He returned his attention to Jack. "You're a lucky man to have found such a bride. I offer you both my felicitations."

"Thank you," Viola said softly.

"And now I must ask that you keep all you have learned today completely confidential."

Viola let go of Jack's hand and sat forward. "We can't say a word? I was going to write a story about this. People should know what is happening."

Orford shook his head firmly. "You cannot. In exchange, Caldwell and his cohorts will not trouble you, and no one will ever know the identity of Mr. Tavistock. Though I do suggest he stop writing for the *Ladies' Gazette* and perhaps relocate to a far-off corner of the country."

"He already has," Viola said with more than a little irritation as her dream of publishing an important news story slipped through her fingers.

"Excellent." Orford stood abruptly. "I think we're finished, then."

Jack rose and helped Viola to her feet. "I suppose we are. Good afternoon." He inclined his head, then escorted Viola from the office and outside to where the coach awaited them.

Raindrops pelted them as they dashed into the vehicle. Once they were inside, Jack let out an oath. Then he apologized. "It's bloody frustrating."

"I know."

He turned toward her on the seat. "I'm so sorry about your story."

"It's all right." It wasn't really, but she'd get over it. "As it happens, I was making notes earlier today about that book I'd like to write."

"Yes, what is this book about?"

"Well now, it's about spies and intrigue and, of course, love."

"Of course." He twined his arms around her and drew her against him. Then he lowered his head and inhaled her scent before kissing her neck. "I much prefer you as Viola."

She tossed his hat to the rear-facing seat and cupped the back of his head, thrusting her fingers into his dark hair. "That's relieving to know."

"Tell me about the love part of your book."

"There's a brilliant man who seeks to help an aspiring reporter with an important news story that will expose corruption at the highest levels of government."

He peered up at her. "The highest levels?"

"That's a new idea that just came to me. I'm still exploring what that means. Perhaps the king—my book can't be based in the present—hires someone to try to assassinate himself in order to gain sympathy for laws that would control the rebellious working classes."

He stared at her, arousal darkening his eyes. "Good God, *you're* brilliant. And terrifying. You can't write a story like that."

She made a disgruntled sound behind pursed lips. "No, I suppose not. But I'll come up with something."

He went back to kissing her neck, his lips trailing down to the hollow, making her shiver. "I am happy to help. Especially with the love part."

"Good. As it happens, that is the part I would like the most help with."

Jack clasped the hem of her gown and swept it up her leg. A moment later, she felt his hand along her inner thigh.

She gasped in surprise and anticipation. "We'll be in Berkeley Square soon."

He rose up next to her as his fingers found her already wet sheath. "Then I shall be quick." He gave her a devilish smile just before he kissed her.

"Not too quick, I hope," she murmured between kisses.

"Don't worry, my love. I shall repeat this and a thousand other things until you tire of me."

She held him fiercely and looked into his eyes with all the love in her heart. "That will never happen."

EPILOGUE

"*A* toast to the bride and groom!" Jack's father raised his glass of champagne at the dinner party hosted by the dowager. Though it hadn't yet been a week since their betrothal, Jack felt as though he were a member of the family.

Eastleigh had welcomed him warmly. He and his wife smiled at Jack from the opposite side of the table. And while the dowager could never be described as warm or welcoming, she was engaging and interested in Jack, both as a person and as her granddaughter's soon-to-be husband.

Soon-to-be.

Tomorrow seemed so far away, and yet it was so close he could taste it. He looked to his left at Viola, who sipped her champagne. Her gaze met his, and in it, he saw the love he felt reflected back at him.

The past several days had been a whirlwind of planning for the wedding and her relocation to his town house. She felt bad leaving her grandmother and had asked him if he would consider relocating here to Berkeley Square next Season. Jack said he'd think about it, but he'd already made up his mind that they should. It seemed he'd fallen in love with *all* the Fairfaxes.

After dinner, they repaired to the drawing room instead of splitting up by sex. Eastleigh clapped Jack on the back as they entered. "Port or brandy?"

"Port, I think. Thank you." Jack accompanied him to the sideboard. "My father will take brandy."

Eastleigh poured the drinks, including three extra glasses of port. "These are for the ladies."

"Viola likes port after dinner?" Jack asked. At Eastleigh's nod, he made a mental note. He still had so much to learn about his bride, and he looked forward to every detail.

Eastleigh picked up two of the glasses for the others, while Jack took the other two. "I wanted to let you know we've also banned Pennington from the Wicked Duke, not that he'll likely show his face anywhere in London for some time."

The resignation from Parliament of Pennington, Caldwell, and Sir Humphrey had eclipsed any scandal surrounding Viola and Jack's hasty nuptials. Viola had done her part to amplify it by including considerable information about them for her monthly column, which she'd amended just before the *Ladies' Gazette* had gone to print. Released yesterday, Tavistock's "farewell" column was all the talk, so much so that the editor had written Viola late today and begged her to reconsider leaving.

As Jack delivered brandy to his father and port to Viola, he remembered the day she'd turned in the column, and smiled.

Viola took the glass from him, brushing her fingers against his. "Why are you grinning?"

"I was just thinking of your editor's face when you turned in your column as yourself instead of Tavistock." Jack hadn't realized a jaw could drop so far.

Having just taken a sip of her port, Viola struggled to swallow and suppress a giggle. "Not fair of you to mention that while I'm drinking."

"You asked why I was smiling. That's why."

"That was a lovely moment, wasn't it?"

"One you wholly deserved." They'd discussed whether she should reveal her true identity to them, but she was confident they wouldn't tell anyone. They were horrified to learn they'd employed a woman and didn't want anyone to know. Jack bent and kissed her temple, then returned to the sideboard to fetch his port.

Eastleigh had also come back for his. "I'm so pleased you and Viola found each other, even if it was a rather unorthodox path." He chuckled. "Not that I am one to talk. It took me ten years to realize what I wanted—what I needed—had been right in front of me all along."

"My father made that mistake," Jack said. "Not that you made a mistake," he added quickly.

Swallowing a sip of port, Eastleigh nodded. "I definitely made a mistake. If I'd realized I loved Isabelle when we'd first met, I could've saved us a great deal of…" He shook his head. "Never mind. It doesn't matter. It only matters that we're together now and forever."

Jack was especially glad he'd decided to ignore his self-imposed timetable for his career and marriage. He could have both. He *would* have both.

"Why are you standing over there muttering between yourselves?" the dowager asked. "Come and sit with us."

They hastened to join the others, Jack settling onto a sofa next to Viola, and Eastleigh doing the same beside his wife.

"We weren't muttering," Eastleigh said. "We were celebrating our good fortune at having found love."

"There is nothing finer than true love," Jack's father said.

Jack looked over at his sire and glimpsed a mist in his eyes he'd rarely seen. He'd been overjoyed to learn Jack was not only getting married but that he'd fallen in love. Honestly, Jack was fairly certain he'd been happier than when Jack had been called to the bar or when he'd been sent to Parliament.

"Hear, hear!" the dowager agreed, and they all drank a toast.

Viola leaned over to Jack and whispered, "I suppose we have scandal to thank."

"I will thank whomever or whatever I must for the rest of my life." He tapped his glass to hers. "To scandal. And to *you*. You've made me the happiest man alive."

"No, you've made me the happiest man—and woman." She winked at him, and he chuckled low in his throat as he kissed her cheek.

He spoke so only she could hear. "If you don so much as a whisker again, I shall have to consider wearing a gown just to spite you."

Her eyes glowed with heat. "I don't care what you wear so long as you take it off."

"Careful, Viola, or you'll cause a scandal right here in your grandmother's drawing room."

She gave him a captivating smile that was quintessentially Viola. "Who said one scandal was ever enough? And no, I am not going to cause a scandal tomorrow by leaving you at the altar. I plan to arrive at the church *early*."

He dipped his gaze over her suggestively. "How early?"

She giggled. "Now, *that* would be a scandal."

"My favorite kind," Jack murmured as he took her hand and pressed a kiss to her wrist. "I promise to fill your days—and nights—with precisely *that*."

What happens when Giles Langford—a penniless daredevil—falls in love with the Duke of Colehaven's sister? Find out in ONE NIGHT TO REMEMBER.

THANK YOU!

Thank you so much for reading One Night of Scandal. I hope you enjoyed it! Don't miss the next book in the Wicked Dukes Club, **ONE NIGHT TO REMEMBER**!

Would you like to know when my next book is available? Sign up for my reader club at http://www.darcyburke.com/readerclub, follow me on social media:

Facebook: http://facebook.com/DarcyBurkeFans
Twitter at @darcyburke
Instagram at darcyburkeauthor
Pinterest at darcyburkewrite

I hope you'll consider leaving a review at your favorite online vendor or networking site!

Follow me on Bookbub to receive updates on pre-orders, new releases, and deals!

Catch up with my other historical series: The Untouchables, Secrets and Scandals, and Legendary Rogues. If you like contemporary romance, I hope you'll check out my Ribbon Ridge series available from Avon Impulse, and the continuation of Ribbon Ridge in So Hot.

I appreciate my readers so much. Thank you, thank you, *thank you*.

ALSO BY DARCY BURKE

Historical Romance

Wicked Dukes Club

One Night for Seduction by Erica Ridley
One Night of Surrender by Darcy Burke
One Night of Passion by Erica Ridley
One Night of Scandal by Darcy Burke
One Night to Remember by Erica Ridley
One Night of Temptation by Darcy Burke

The Spitfire Society

Never Have I Ever With a Duke
A Duke is Never Enough
A Duke Will Never Do

The Untouchables

The Forbidden Duke
The Duke of Daring
The Duke of Deception
The Duke of Desire
The Duke of Defiance
The Duke of Danger
The Duke of Ice
The Duke of Ruin
The Duke of Lies
The Duke of Seduction

The Duke of Kisses
The Duke of Distraction

Secrets and Scandals

Her Wicked Ways
His Wicked Heart
To Seduce a Scoundrel
To Love a Thief (a novella)
Never Love a Scoundrel
Scoundrel Ever After

Legendary Rogues

Lady of Desire
Romancing the Earl
Lord of Fortune
Captivating the Scoundrel

Contemporary Romance

Ribbon Ridge

Where the Heart Is (a prequel novella)
Only in My Dreams
Yours to Hold
When Love Happens
The Idea of You
When We Kiss
You're Still the One

Ribbon Ridge: So Hot

So Good

So Right
So Wrong

THE JEWELS OF HISTORICAL
ROMANCE

The Jewels are my sisters in historical romance: *New York Times* and *USA Today* bestselling authors who sparkle! Download our two boxed sets for just 99c each so you can meet the rest of the Jewels...

Fabulous Firsts: The Blue Collection - 6 novels for just 99c

Fabulous Firsts: The Red Collection - 6 novels for just 99c!

Enter our monthly contest at:
JewelsofHistoricalRomance.com

And join the Jewels Salon on Facebook!

ABOUT THE AUTHOR

Darcy Burke is the USA Today Bestselling Author of sexy, emotional historical and contemporary romance. Darcy wrote her first book at age 11, a happily ever after about a swan addicted to magic and the female swan who loved him, with exceedingly poor illustrations. Join her Reader Club at http://www.darcyburke.com/readerclub.

A native Oregonian, Darcy lives on the edge of wine country with her guitar-strumming husband, their two hilarious kids who seem to have inherited the writing gene. They're a crazy cat family with two Bengal cats, a small, fame-seeking cat named after a fruit, and an older rescue Maine Coon who is the master of chill and five a.m. serenading. In her "spare" time Darcy is a serial volunteer enrolled in a 12-step program where one learns to say "no," but she keeps having to start over. Her happy places are Disneyland and Labor Day weekend at the Gorge. Visit Darcy online at http://www.darcyburke.com and follow her social media: Facebook at http://www.facebook.com/darcyburkefans, Twitter @darcyburke at http://www.twitter.com/darcyburke, Instagram at http://www.instagram/darcyburkeauthor, and Pinterest at http://www. pinterest.com/darcyburkewrite.